"You're still bleeding."

Arianna moved under a group of mountain alders. "Sit while I clean your cuts."

"There's no time," Brody said. "The farther away from the cabin we are, the safer we'll be."

Still, she wiped the cuts on his cheek and he stayed still, his gaze fixed on her. Though she tried to ignore it, her stomach twisted. His eyes seemed to bore deep into her—as though trying to discover her innermost secrets. She had no intention of sharing those with him or anyone else.

"Close your eyes." She dabbed at the cut above his eye, and slowly the knots unraveled in her gut. With his eyes closed, she got a chance to scrutinize him. There was a strength and ruggedness to him that told her he knew how to take care of himself. That appealed to her. Too much.

She needed to squash that feeling. Caring about the person protecting you wasn't wise.

Now, if only her h

Books by Margaret Daley

Love Inspired Suspense

So Dark the Night
Vanished
Buried Secrets
Don't Look Back
Forsaken Canyon
What Sarah Saw
Poisoned Secrets
Cowboy Protector
Christmas Peril
   "Merry Mayhem"
§*Christmas Bodyguard*
Trail of Lies
§*Protecting Her Own*
§*Hidden in the Everglades*
§*Christmas Stalking*
Detection Mission
§*Guarding the Witness*

*The Ladies of
   Sweetwater Lake
†Fostered by Love
††Helping Hands
   Homeschooling
**A Town Called Hope
§Guardians, Inc.

Love Inspired

*Gold in the Fire
*A Mother for Cindy
*Light in the Storm
   The Cinderella Plan
*When Dreams Come True
   Hearts on the Line
*Tidings of Joy
   Heart of the Amazon
†Once Upon a Family
†Heart of the Family
†Family Ever After
   A Texas Thanksgiving
†Second Chance Family
†Together for the Holidays
††Love Lessons
††Heart of a Cowboy
††A Daughter for Christmas
**His Holiday Family
**A Love Rekindled
**A Mom's New Start

MARGARET DALEY

feels she has been blessed. She has been married more than thirty years to her husband, Mike, whom she met in college. He is a terrific support and her best friend. They have one son, Shaun. Margaret has been writing for many years and loves to tell a story. When she was a little girl, she would play with her dolls and make up stories about their lives. Now she writes these stories down. She especially enjoys weaving stories about families and how faith in God can sustain a person when things get tough. When she isn't writing, she is fortunate to be a teacher for students with special needs. Margaret has taught for more than twenty years and loves working with her students. She has also been a Special Olympics coach and has participated in many sports with her students.

GUARDING THE WITNESS

MARGARET DALEY

HARLEQUIN® LOVE INSPIRED® SUSPENSE

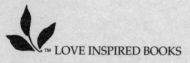

™ LOVE INSPIRED BOOKS

ISBN-13: 978-0-373-67562-3

GUARDING THE WITNESS

www.LoveInspiredBooks.com

Printed in U.S.A.

Trust in the Lord with all thine heart; and lean not unto thine own understanding. In all thy ways acknowledge Him, and He shall direct thy paths.
—*Proverbs* 3:5,6

To all my readers—
I appreciate you for reading my books. Thank you.

PROLOGUE

Bodyguard Arianna Jackson flexed her fingers over her holstered Glock at her side, ready to draw at a second's notice if she sensed her client, Esther Perkins, was in danger. She cased the garage as she and Esther moved toward the door to the utility room of her client's house.

"Every time we come back from my lawyer's office, all I want to do is sleep for the next week," Esther said with a deep sigh. "At least we didn't stay long this time. I'm glad to be home early. If my husband had bothered to show up, I'd still be there."

Esther's lawyer had refused to conduct the meeting without Thomas Perkins present to finalize the details of the divorce. Therefore the meeting was cut short, actually never started. That was fine with Arianna. Whenever they left the house, the chances went up that her client would be hurt by her husband, whom Esther had found out was part of a huge crime syndicate in Alaska. "Hang back until I check each room."

"As soon as this divorce is over with, I'm getting as far away from my soon-to-be ex as I can." The forty-five-year-old hugged her arms to her chest and stopped right behind Arianna. "I won't live in this kind of fear. He's a violent, horrible man."

Arianna unlocked the door into the house and eased it open, listening for any abnormal sounds. Silence greeted her, and the urge to relax her vigilance tempted her for only a second. She'd learned the hard way never to do that while working as a bodyguard. She had her old injury to her shoulder—a bullet that went all the way through—to remind her.

When she was satisfied it was safe for Esther to enter, she motioned to the woman then trekked toward the kitchen, making a visual sweep of the room before moving into it.

A sound, like a muffled thud, penetrated the quiet. Arianna immediately pulled her gun from its holster and chambered a round, then swung around and put her finger to her mouth to indicate no talking. Waving her hand toward the pantry, she herded her client toward it. At the door she whispered into Esther's ear. "Stay in here. I'm locking the door. Stay back away from it. I'm checking the sound out. You know the drill."

With a shaky hand, Esther dug into her purse for her cell to call 911 if she thought it was needed.

And because her client didn't always do what she was supposed to unless Arianna spelled it out—and because there was a way to unlock the pantry from the inside—she added, "Don't leave the pantry until I tell you to."

Her blue eyes huge, Esther nodded, all color draining from her face.

With her client secured—at least as much as she could be with a possible intruder in the house—Arianna crept forward. She scanned each room as she made her way through the lower level. Another dull thump echoed through the air. She knew that sound—a silencer. Coming from the library. A muted scream followed almost immediately. Every sense heightened to a razor-sharp alertness.

The couple who lived here with Esther was gone for a few days to a funeral. No one should have been in the place. Increasing her pace, she covered the length of the hallway in a few seconds and flattened herself against the wall to one side of the door that was ajar.

Peering through the slice of space into the library, she spied a large man about six and a half feet tall standing over Thomas Perkins, who was bound to a chair with his hands tied behind his back and a gag in his mouth. He bled from the shoulder and thigh—a lot. Esther's husband tried to scooch back from the towering man, moaning through the cloth stuffed in his mouth, his eyes dilated with fear.

The assailant leaned down and removed the gag. "No whining. Just tell me where the ledger is or the next shot will be in your heart."

"There isn't one," Thomas Perkins said between coughs, still trying to move away from the man.

"Yeah, right. I know you have one in case you needed to use it against me. Your mistake was talking about it to the wrong person."

She wasn't paid to protect her client's soon-to-be ex-husband, but she couldn't stand by and watch an assailant murder him. Fortifying herself with a steadying breath, Arianna nudged the door open, pointed the gun at the attacker's heart and said, "Drop the weapon or I'll shoot."

The large man's hand inched upward.

"I don't play around. I'll only have to shoot you once to kill you instantly."

The man's fiery gaze bored through Arianna. "You've just made the biggest mistake of your life."

ONE

Two months later, a helicopter banked to the left and descended toward the clearing where Deputy U.S. Marshal Brody Callahan's new assignment, Arianna Jackson, was being guarded by three marshals. His team would relieve them, so he used his vantage point above the forest to check out the area. Knowing the terrain that surrounded the safe house had saved his life several times. The cabin backed up against a medium-size mountain range on the north and west while the other two sides were made up of a wall of spruces, pines, hemlocks and other varieties of trees that stretched out for miles. A rugged land—manageable only as long as the weather cooperated. It was the end of July, but it had been known to snow at that time in Alaska near the Artic Circle. He had to be prepared for all contingencies.

As they dropped toward the clearing, Deputy U.S. Marshal Ted Banks came out of the cabin, staying back by the door, his hand hovering near his gun in his holster. Alert. Ted was a good marshal Brody had worked with before.

The helicopter's landing skids connected with the ground, jolting Brody slightly. Over the whirring noise of the rotors, he yelled to the pilot, "This shouldn't take long."

With duffel bags in hand, Brody jumped to the rocky earth closest to the cabin while his two partners exited from the other side. Brody ran toward Ted, who held out his hand and said in a booming voice, "Glad to see you."

"Ready to see your wife, are you?"

"Yep. I hope you've honed your Scrabble skills. This one is ruthless when it comes to the game. I'm going to brush up on my vocabulary with a dictionary before I play her again."

"I've read her file." Arianna Jackson was the star witness for the trial of Joseph Rainwater, the head of a large crime syndicate in Alaska, because she'd witnessed Rainwater killing Thomas Perkins. The man had bled out before the EMTs arrived.

"Doesn't do her justice. I don't have anything to add to my earlier phone report this morning. C'mon. I'll introduce you two." Ted peered over Brody's shoulder at his partners, Kevin Laird and Mark Baylor, approaching them while carrying a bag and three boxes of provisions. Ted nodded to them before turning to open the door.

As Brody entered, he panned the rustic interior with a high ceiling, noting where the few windows were located, the large fireplace against the back wall, the hallway that led to the two bedrooms and the kitchen area off the living room. Three duffel bags sat by the door. Then his gaze connected with the witness he was to protect.

Arianna Jackson.

Tall, with white-blond hair and cool gray eyes, she resembled a Nordic princess. Still, he could tell she was very capable of taking care of herself from the way she carried herself, right down to the sharp perusal she gave him. From what he'd read, Ms. Jackson had been a good bodyguard caught in a bad situation. Her life would never be the same after this.

She tossed the dish towel she held onto the kitchen counter, never taking her gaze off him. She assessed and catalogued him, not one emotion on her face to indicate what she had decided about him. That piqued his interest.

"These three are our replacements—Brody Callahan, Kevin Laird and Mark Baylor. This is Arianna Jackson," Ted said. Then he headed toward the door, the tension from his body fading with each step. "It's been quiet this past week except for a pesky mama bear and her cubs." He shoved into Brody's hand a sheet of paper with instructions on how to avoid a bear encounter.

"Good. Have you seen anyone in the area?"

"Nope, just the wildlife. We are, even for Alaska, out in the boonies," Ted said, giving him a salute. "Hope the next time I see you is in Anchorage. Goodbye, Arianna."

Brody looked from Ted, almost fleeing, to Carla Matthews not far behind him, to Dan Mitchell, the third Deputy U.S. Marshal on team number one, who would be on vacation on a beach in Hawaii. Brody clenched his jaw, curling his fingers around the handle of his bag so tightly his skin stretched taut over his knuckles. Carla shot him a piercing glance before disappearing outside. Slowly, Brody released his grip on his duffel bag, and it dropped to the floor with a thud.

Good thing Ted and Dan worked with Carla. He had once and wouldn't again. He'd learned the hard way to never get involved with a colleague. In fact, she'd been one of the reasons he'd transferred to Alaska from Los Angeles. It had been a hard shock to find out she'd been recruited to be on the detail protecting Arianna Jackson. At least she would return to L.A. when this trial was over.

Brody swung his attention to his witness,

who watched team one leave. These assignments were never easy on anyone involved. The pressure was intense. Never able to let down your guard. And with Ms. Jackson the stakes were even higher because Joseph Rainwater was determined his crime syndicate would find her and take her out, along with anyone else in their way. And the man had the resources and money to carry out that threat.

Her gaze linked with his. "The bedroom on the right is where you all can bunk," Ms. Jackson said in a no-nonsense voice as she rotated back to finish drying the few dishes in the drain board.

Patience, Lord. I'm pretty sure I'm going to need every ounce of it this next week. He was guarding a woman who was used to guarding others. He doubted she would like to follow orders when she was used to giving them.

Brody nodded to Kevin and Mark to go ahead and take their duffel bags into the room assigned to them by their witness. Then Brody covered the distance between him and Ms. Jackson. "We need to talk."

She turned her head and tilted it. One eyebrow rose. "We do? Am I going to get the lecture about not going outside, to follow all your ord—directions?"

"No, because you guard people for a living

and you know what to do. But I do have some news I thought you deserved to know."

Her body stiffening, she faced him fully, her shoulders thrust back as though she were at attention. "What?"

"Esther Perkins is missing."

Arianna clenched her hands. "No one would tell me anything about Esther other than she was being taken care of. She didn't witness the murder. She couldn't testify about it. What happened?"

"Rainwater thought she might know something concerning the ledger and went after her. Or rather he sent a couple of his men since Rainwater is sitting in jail. We moved her out of state while she tried to help us find that ledger even from long distance."

"So the police never could locate it?"

"No. They figure it has to be important since Rainwater personally killed a man over it. Usually others do his dirty work. The ledger probably details his contacts and operation. Thomas Perkins was in a position to know that information."

"So how did Esther go missing? Maybe she just left the program." She knew that was wishful thinking. When she'd stressed the importance of staying put, the woman always did.

She'd been scared of her husband and now knowing who he'd worked for she was even more afraid.

"No, the Deputy U.S. Marshal running the case said it didn't look like she had. It had been obvious there had been a fight. There was blood found on the carpet. It was her type."

Her fingernails dug into her palms. Anger tangled with sadness and won. "She didn't have a detail on her?"

"She was relocated with a new identity thousands of miles away."

"Then maybe you have a leak somewhere." She pivoted back to the sink, her stomach roiling with rage that a good woman was probably dead. This all wouldn't have happened if they had stayed at Esther lawyer's office for another hour or so. Why, God? It had tested her faith; and now with the Rainwater situation her doubts concerning the Lord had multiplied. As had her doubts about herself.

For the past four years she'd worked for Guardians, Inc., a group of female bodyguards run by Kyra Hunt. In that time, she had seen some vile people who would hurt others without hesitation. She'd thought she had been tough enough for the job, especially with all she'd seen in the military in the Middle East during several tours. Now she was wondering if this was a good time to change jobs.

The continual silence from Brody after her accusation made her slant a look over her shoulder. A frown slashed across his face, the first sign of emotion from him.

His gaze roped hers. "It's more likely Esther contacted someone when she shouldn't. Let slip where she was. We've never lost a witness *if* they followed the rules."

"Take it from me—this isn't easy to do. Walk away from everyone you know and start a new life. I can't even call my mother or anyone else from my past." Arianna had always called her mom at least once a week, even when she was on a job, to make sure everything was going all right, wishfully hoping one of those times her father would talk with her. He never had, which broke her heart each time. Not being able to at least talk with her mom, except that one time right after the incident in the Perkinses' library, added family heartache on top of everything else.

"All I can tell you is that the U.S. Marshals Service is doing everything they can to locate Mrs. Perkins."

Left unsaid was "dead or alive." She closed her eyes, weariness attacking her from all sides. Since coming to the cabin, she hadn't slept more than a few hours here and there. The marshals had moved her from Anchorage because they'd worried the safe house had been compromised. If that place had been, why not this one?

That question plagued her every waking moment. It was hard to rest when she didn't know the people involved in her protection. When she did lie down, she'd managed to catch some sleep because she had her gun with her. She'd brought extra money, a switchblade and her gun without the marshals' knowledge. In case something went down, she wanted to be prepared. That was the only way she would agree to all of this. She would see to her own protection. She didn't trust anyone but herself to keep her alive.

Not even God anymore. That thought crept into her mind and prodded her memories. She wouldn't think about the reason she'd left the army, much to her brothers' and father's dismay. But how could she trust again when one of her team had sold her out? In the end it wasn't the Lord who had saved her. She'd saved herself.

That was when she'd vowed to protect others. She never wanted another to live in fear the way she had—scared she would go to prison for a crime she hadn't committed.

She turned toward the marshal, appreciating what her clients must have felt when she'd guarded them and told them what to do. "Promise me you'll let me know if you all find Esther. She was my client. I feel responsible for her."

"You did everything you could. If you hadn't been there, she would have been dead next to her husband."

"And now she may be dead, her body somewhere no one has found yet. May never find."

"Yes," Deputy U.S. Marshal Brody Callahan said over the sound of the helicopter taking off.

The blunt reality of what might have happened to Esther, and still could happen, hung in the air between Arianna and the marshal. She went back to drying the lunch dishes. Anything to keep her occupied. If this inactivity didn't end soon, she might go running through the woods screaming.

Mark Baylor, the oldest of the three marshals, with a touch of gray at his temples, strode to the door. "I'm gonna take a stroll around the perimeter."

Usually one marshal stayed outside while two were inside—often one of them taking his turn sleeping. That was the way it had been set up with Ted and his team.

"Do you need any help?" The deep, husky voice of Brody Callahan, the marshal who seemed to be in charge, broke into her thoughts.

"With cleaning up?" she asked, surprised by the question.

"Yes."

She glanced back at him. Six inches taller than her five-feet-eleven frame, Brody carried himself with confidence, which in its own way did ease her anxiety about her situation. His figure, with not an ounce of fat on him and a broad, muscular chest, spoke of a man that kept himself in shape. "I've got it under control." *About the only thing in my life that is.*

"We equally share the duties while we're here."

"That's good to know. I don't cook."

"You don't?"

She finished drying the last plate. "Never had a reason to learn. I went from living at home with my family to the army. Then when I started working for Guardians, Inc., I found myself on assignment most of the time with wealthy clients who had cooks." She shrugged. "The short amount of time I was in Dallas I ate out or ate frozen dinners."

"That's okay. I love to cook," Kevin Laird, the youngest of the marshals, announced as he came into the living room.

Brody chuckled. "That's why I like to team up with Kevin when I can. He can make the most boring food taste decent."

"Good. I'm not averse to edible food." Arianna moved out of the kitchen area, trying to decide what she should do next. *Let's see...*

maybe a crossword puzzle. Or better yet, soli- taire. She still had at least fifty varieties to work her way through. The thought of more days like the past week heightened her boredom level to critical.

She began to pace from one of the few win- dows, drapes pulled, to the hearth. It was empty and cold. They couldn't have a fire even at night when it did get chilly since it indicated someone was at the place. She counted her steps, men- tally mapping out an escape route if she needed it. Her thoughts were interrupted when Kevin spoke up from the kitchen.

"This is a park ranger's cabin. Where's the guy that usually stays here?"

"On an extended vacation." Brody prowled the living room in a different direction from her.

"Does he know we're using it?" Arianna asked as she peeked out the window. The pre- vious set of marshals had told her about the cabin, but only now had she started to wonder what the tenant had been told.

"No, the cabin belongs to the park service. No one knows you're here or that the U.S. Mar- shals Service is using it to protect a witness. A bogus agency has rented it while the park ranger is gone. They think we're here on vaca- tion." Brody parted the drapes and looked out the only other window in the room.

"When's he due back?" Arianna spied a bull moose in the thick of the trees. Seeing the beautiful animals was the one thrill she got being where she was. She loved animals, but because of her job, she hadn't been able to have any—not even a goldfish.

"Not for two more weeks. Do you see it?" Brody's gaze captured hers, nodding in the direction of the moose.

"He's beautiful. I wish I could go outside and take a picture. I took the Perkins assignment because it was in Alaska. After I finished guarding her, I was going to take a long overdue vacation and do some touring of the countryside up here. The most exciting thing that's happened to me this week was the helicopter ride to this cabin. Breathtaking scenery."

"Don't even think about going outside to snap a picture."

She held up her hands, palms outward. "I thought you said I knew the drill and didn't need to hear your spiel."

"I've changed my mind. You sound like a bored witness. That kind can do things to get themselves killed."

"I am bored. I don't even have the luxury of a television set. Most of the time I don't watch it, but I'm desperate. How in the world do you do this job after job?"

"I'm on an assignment to keep you safe. I can't let down my guard ever or allow for any distractions. You should know what that means."

His intense, dark brown eyes drilling into her exemplified strong will and fierce determination—traits she shared. He was a person she should be able to identify with if she stopped feeling sorry for herself—something she rarely did. But she hated change, and the changing of the guard not half an hour ago bothered her more than she'd realized. She now had to get to know her three new guards, and she still couldn't shake the thought that her safe house in Anchorage might have been compromised. She'd feel better if two of the female bodyguards from Guardians, Inc. were here with her instead. She knew where they were coming from.

"How about chess?" Kevin asked from the kitchen area, gesturing to the chess set perched on a shelf, while Brody crossed to the door.

"I don't play it. Where are you going?" she asked Brody as he opened the door.

"Outside. I'm relieving Mark."

"But he just left."

"Yeah, I know."

"Can I come with you?" the imp in her asked. He frowned and left, the door slamming shut.

"Ms. Jackson, I can teach you to play chess.

It'll take your mind off what's going on." Kevin moved into the main part of the room.

"Nothing is going on. That's the problem." She strode toward the table and took a chair. "Sure. I might as well learn." She checked her watch. Noon. It was going to be another long day.

Finishing his last trip around the perimeter of the cabin, Brody took a deep breath of the fresh air, laced with the scent of earth and trees, then mounted the steps to the porch. When he reached the door to the ranger's cabin, he panned the small clearing. Nearing midnight, it was still light outside. The temperature began to drop as the sun finally started its descent. When moving to Alaska, the only thing he really had to adjust to was the long daylight hours in summer and equally long nighttime ones in winter. At least in Anchorage where he was living it was farther south and the days and nights didn't get as skewed as they did up here nearer the Arctic Circle.

Inside the cabin, he left the shotgun by the door for Kevin, who was relieving him on patrol. He turned to find Arianna sitting on the couch, staring at him. Her gray eyes with a hint of blue reminded him of the lake he'd flown over this morning.

"Did you see the mama bear that's been hanging around the cabin lately?" she asked and went back to playing solitaire.

"No. Where's Kevin?"

"Right here. Sorry. I figured I needed a jacket since the sun was going down." Kevin picked up the shotgun and exited the cabin.

"So it's just you and me since Mark is taking his turn sleeping."

For a second he thought he saw a teasing gleam in her eyes before she averted her gaze to study the spread of cards on the coffee table in front of her. He sat in a chair across from her. "Have you won any games?"

"Two probably out of fifty." She raised her head. "Wanna play Scrabble?"

"I've been warned about you and Scrabble."

"I took you for a man who likes a good challenge." A full-fledged smile encompassed her whole face.

"And baiting me guarantees you'll have an opponent."

"Yep, kinda hard playing Scrabble with yourself. No challenge really."

"You're on. Where's the game?"

Arianna gestured toward the bookcase behind him. "I think I'll leave the ranger who lives here a thank-you note. I don't know what I would have done without some of his games.

I brought a deck of cards and some books, but I went through the books in the first four days and I'm sick of playing solitaire. Do you have any idea when I'll get to testify and can move back to civilization?"

"No. Rainwater's attorney gets big bucks to delay the trial as long as he can."

"Because he's got people out there looking for me."

"Yes, you know the score. If you testify, he'll most likely go down for murder. Without finding the ledger Rainwater killed Perkins over, you're the main witness in his trial. Without you, he'd probably get acquitted, if they even went ahead with the trial."

"Something very incriminating must be in the ledger Rainwater was looking for."

"Perkins kept the books for Rainwater. The public set has been sanitized not to include anything incriminating. We think Perkins kept a second ledger with all the dirt on the man. As you know, risky for Perkins to do, but it could be invaluable to us. Rainwater has gone to great lengths to find it."

"We can't afford for people like him to win. I'm even more determined to testify."

"And he's as determined to stop you." Brody rose and retrieved the box with the Scrabble game in it, then laid the board and tiles out on the coffee table. When he sat again, he pulled his chair closer. "Ready to get trounced?"

"Is that any way to speak to a poor defenseless witness?" Arianna said as she laid down seven tiles for a score of seventy-six points.

He looked down at his letters and could only come up with a twelve-point word. Now he was beginning to understand what Ted meant. Forty minutes later it was confirmed. She was *very good* at Scrabble.

"What do you do? Study the dictionary like Ted threatened?"

"No. Don't have to. I have a photographic memory, and I enjoy reading a lot. Once I see something, I remember it."

"So that's how you could give such a detailed description of what went down the day Thomas Perkins was murdered."

"The gift has helped me in my job. When I go on a new assignment, I case the house or wherever I'm staying with the client so I can pull up the layout in a hurry in my mind. It has helped me on more than one occasion, especially in the dark." She gathered up the tiles and began putting them into the box.

"I do something similar although I don't have a photographic memory."

One corner of her mouth lifted. "I consider it one of the weapons in my arsenal."

He laughed, folding the game board and laying it on top of the tiles. "That's an interesting way to put it."

Arianna yawned. "I'd better call it a night and try to sleep."

"Are you having problems sleeping?"

"Yes. Wouldn't you if you were in my position, with all that's been going on?"

"We're guarding you. You don't have to be alert and on the job."

"Actually the quiet is too quiet. I'm glad to hear an occasional animal call in the night."

"I grew up in New York City. The first few years after I left I had the hardest time with the silence at nighttime. Until I was assigned to L.A., I was located in smaller cities. Now when I get it, I love it. My house is outside Anchorage where it's—"

A blast from a shotgun exploded in the air.

As Arianna dove over the back of the sofa with a wall of the cabin behind her, Brody moved toward the door. Another gunshot sound reverberated through the quiet.

Mark rushed down the hallway, weapon drawn. "What's going on?"

"Stay with Ms. Jackson. I'll go check."

Suddenly there was a rattling on the window on the left side of the room as if someone or something was tearing at the screen.

Brody moved toward it. A roar split the air as he opened the blinds to find a grizzly bear attacking the window. The screen hung in metal shreds from its frame. The huge animal batted it away, only a pane of glass now between him and the bear.

"Stay put, Arianna." Brody signaled for Mark to keep an eye on the window where the bear was.

Where is Kevin? His heart pounding, Brody charged toward the exit, knowing his Glock might not be enough to stop a bear coming at him or Kevin. In the gray light of an Alaskan night this far north, he saw his partner backing around the corner of the cabin while squeezing off another shot into the air.

"I'm behind you, Kevin," Brody said as he approached him.

The tense set to his partner's body relaxed. "She's leaving. Finally. When I was making my rounds, two cubs came out of the woods close to where I was. Mama bear followed not five seconds later. I tried not to show any fear and backed away. She came toward me—not charging, but making sure she was between her cubs and me. When I fired my first warning shot in the air, both of the cubs ran into the woods. She didn't."

Kevin kept his gaze fixed on the departing

bear while Brody watched the front of the cabin. When the threat disappeared into the woods, they both headed for the porch.

"Good thing she doesn't know how to open doors or windows. It took three shots to scare her off," Kevin said, then positioned himself by the steps.

"She's establishing her territory. Next time stay closer to the cabin and don't play around with a grizzly sow and her cubs. They are very protective of their babies."

"Believe me I'll stay glued to this place. I don't want to tangle with one of them."

"I'll be turning in soon. Mark will be on duty in the cabin. I'll relieve you in five hours." When Brody reentered the cabin, Arianna stood behind the couch. "What part of get down do you not understand?"

"The last order you gave me was stay put." She pointed to the floor. "I stayed put. Besides, Mark was here."

Brody shook his head. "I guess I'll have to spell it out for you next time."

"There's gonna be a next time with that bear?"

"If she's hungry enough or we threaten her cubs. Obviously she didn't like Kevin near her cubs or shooting his gun—even in the air."

"Oh, good. If she comes back to us, I'll get to take a photo."

"Photo? Of a bear charging you?"

"No. Don't you remember you've ordered me to stay in the cabin? I'll be watching from the window. No charging bear will be coming at me. Now that's not to say she won't come after you or your partners…"

He chuckled. "I'll make sure I'm not your model for that picture."

Mark laughed, too. "I'm going back to bed for the little time I have left. I'll leave you two to hash things out."

As Mark left, Arianna said, "When I finished a job in Africa, I went on a photo safari. One of the rare vacations I gave myself. After this job I was going to take a second vacation and see some of the wildlife. I don't think that's going to work out unless I can get the wildlife to come to me."

"Give me the camera. I'll take a picture for you."

"Not the same thing. Besides, the bear is long gone by now. At least I hope so." Another yawn escaped Arianna. "That's my cue to say good-night."

"Good night. Mark will be back in here—" he checked his watch "—in an hour."

"Sleep tight then."

"Don't you mean sleep light? After all, I am guarding you."

"Every bodyguard has to grab some good sleep if he or she is going to do a good job. And believe me, I want you to do a good job protecting me."

He studied her body language as she said those words. "I think you believe what you said, but you also believe you can take care of yourself."

She smirked. "I'm gonna have to work on fooling you better."

"No one, not even myself, is invincible. We all need help from time to time."

"And who do you turn to?"

"God and my partner on the job. In that order."

Her eyes widened for a second before she rotated toward the hallway and headed toward her bedroom.

Brody watched her leave, flashes of his own experience questioning God's intention going through his mind. He'd been the lead marshal on an assignment in Los Angeles. The witness he'd been guarding ended up being gunned down on the way to the courthouse because the cell phone in his pocket was used to track his movements.

Brody shook the memory from his mind. That was the past. He couldn't change it, but he could learn from it. Now Brody needed to be the sharpest marshal he could be. He wasn't going to lose another witness on his team.

When Mark relieved him later, Brody strode toward his bedroom. His glance strayed toward Arianna's closed door. She was an interesting woman whose life would never be the same. How would *he* deal with giving up all he knew and starting over?

Her earlier adrenaline rush finally subsiding, Arianna removed her Glock from under the mattress and put it on the bedside table within easy reach. That was the only way she would be able to get any kind of sleep. When she lay down and closed her eyes, the image of Brody Callahan, laughing at some of the words she came up with, popped onto the screen of her mind. Though she'd won the Scrabble match, he hadn't gone down without a fight, challenging a few of the words she'd used that he didn't know. But mostly she remembered his good nature at losing to her.

Sleep faded the picture of her and Brody facing each other over the Scrabble board and whisked her into a dream world that evolved into a nightmare she hadn't had in a year—one where she was shoved into a prison cell. As she swept around to rush out, the bars slammed shut, the sound clanging through her mind.

The noise jerked her awake. Her eyelids flew open. Silence greeted her and calmed her racing heart.

Until she heard a muffled thud—as though a silencer had been fired.

TWO

The distinctive sound of a gun with a silencer discharging nearby yanked Brody from sleep. As he rolled out of bed, he grabbed his Glock from his bedside table. Kevin and Mark didn't have silencers on their weapons, which meant someone had made it inside. Had there been more than one shot? Since he hadn't heard his partners' guns going off, he had to assume something happened to them. What had he slept through?

Hurrying toward his door, he shoved deep down the thought of the worst occurring. He couldn't afford to be sidetracked. He had to be as detached and professional as possible. There would be time later for emotion.

He eased open the door a crack and listened. Silence ruled. For a second he wondered if he'd dreamed hearing the sound. Hoped he had. Then a whisper of a noise alerted him to Arianna easing her door open slightly. His gaze seized hers, and he knew she'd heard the same thing. It wasn't a dream.

The cabin had been compromised. Fortifying himself with a deep breath, he swung the door open wide and stepped out into the hallway with his Glock pointed toward the living room. To his side he noticed Arianna stepping into the corridor. He shook his head. She ignored him and continued out into the hall with a gun in her hand.

He shouldn't be surprised she'd brought her own gun to the cabin. He would have in her place. But still he frowned and tried to convey silently that she get back into her room.

A low moan coming from the living room refocused his full attention on the threat in the cabin. Short of handcuffing her to her bed, she would be backing him up. Waving her behind him, he crept down the hallway. At least this way he could shield her.

Toward the entrance into the living room, he slowed and flattened himself against the wall then inched forward. Much to his dismay Arianna copied him but on the other side of the corridor. She brought her Glock up, both hands clasping it. She ignored the displeasure he knew showed on his face, her gaze trained on the living area.

At the moment, survival was the most important objective. He gave up trying to have Arianna hang back. He knew from all the reports she was very capable of handling herself so he indicated she cover the left side of the room while he took the right. They entered in unison.

One large man was dragging Mark's body out of sight while Brody glimpsed another intruder by the front door.

"Drop your weapons," Brody said, preparing for them not to obey.

The guy moving Mark ducked down behind the kitchen counter while the one at the door raised his gun and fired. Arianna squeezed off a round at the shooter then stepped back behind the wall into the hallway for cover. While that intruder went down with a wound to the chest, Brody dived behind the couch and crawled forward to get a better angle on the attacker in the kitchen. He popped up at the same time Brody aimed his Glock and took the man out. The thud resounded through the cabin when he crashed to the floor.

Brody rose, swinging around in a full circle to make sure there were no more assailants in the cabin. Arianna had disappeared down the hallway, and the sound he heard now of doors opening and closing as she checked each room raised his admiration for the lady's skills.

When Arianna came back, he said, "I'm

checking outside. There may be more. I need to see where Kevin is. You'll have to see if Mark is alive. From his injury, I don't think he is." But he prayed his partner was. And Kevin.

"Be careful. Sending two men to kill four doesn't make sense."

"I know. That's what concerns me." As he approached the intruder by the door, he leaned over and felt for a pulse. "This one is dead."

Arianna arrived in the kitchen. "So is this guy."

He opened the door. "What about Mark?"

Ducking down behind the counter, Arianna answered in a heavy voice, "Dead."

That was what he'd thought. With a head wound Mark hadn't had a chance to get a shot off. And to get into the cabin they had to go through Kevin. A young marshal with only a year's experience. Again he reminded himself to tamp down his emotions. Later he could mourn the dead. His only goal was to protect Arianna.

"Lock this after I leave." Dread at what he would find blanketed him as he slipped through the front door out onto the porch. Already the night sky started growing light as sunrise neared at four-thirty.

No one was on the porch. Alert, every muscle taut with tension, Brody descended the steps and slinked toward the left side of the cabin.

When he rounded the corner, a man plowed into him, sending him flying back. Brody managed to keep a grip on his gun even while his arms flung out. The impact with the ground caused the air to swoosh from him. The bulky assailant crushed him into the dirt, sitting on him, knees pinning down his arms and fists pounding into Brody's upper body and face. Stars swam before Brody's eyes. From deep inside him he drew on his reserve, fueled by a spurt of adrenaline. He was the only thing standing between Arianna and death.

Between punches Brody sucked in a shallow breath, laced with the scent of sweat, then poured what strength he had into freeing one of his pinned arms. When he did, Brody cuffed the brute on the side of the head with his Glock. The man's drive slowed. Brody struck him again with the butt of the weapon.

His assailant growled and swiveled his upper body, grasping the hand that held the weapon. His attacker wrestled Brody for the gun, trying to twist his arm—possibly to break it. The Glock hovered between them. Brody focused all his will on an effort to regain control of the weapon. His chest burned with the lack of oxygen. The gun wavered inches from Brody, the barrel slowly turning toward him. A dark haze edged into his mind. Brody sent up a silent plea to God, and with a last burst of strength, he halted the Glock's momentum, then he began turning the end toward his assailant's torso.

Brody pulled his finger around the trigger with the man's hand still covering his. Brody stared into his attacker's dark eyes as the bullet exploded from the weapon, striking his assailant's chest. He jerked then slumped over, pinning Brody to the ground.

His ears ringing, the scent of gunpowder filling his nostrils, he shoved the man off him and scrambled away, never taking his eyes off his attacker. In the dim light of predawn he felt for a pulse. Gone. He checked the man's pockets for ID. There was none, but he found a switchblade with blood on it. Brody searched the area.

What happened here? Where is Kevin?

Tension stretched every nerve to beyond its limit. Rising, Brody kept scanning the terrain as he circled the cabin, using the shadows to cover his presence as much as possible. By the time he reached the porch again, he was even more confused by what had happened. Kevin was nowhere he could see, and he hadn't encountered anyone or anything else suspicious.

When he knocked on the door, he said, "It's Brody." He noticed the drapes over the window move, then a few seconds later the click on the lock sounded in the quiet. Too quiet. No birds tweeted. No howls of the wolves he'd heard earlier. The hairs on his nape stood up.

How did the assailants arrive? Not by helicopter. He would have heard that. By four-wheel drive? By foot?

The door swung open. Arianna took one look at him and dragged him inside. "I hope the other guy looks worse."

"He's dead. I can't find Kevin. At least he's not near the cabin or in the open area."

"I almost came out when I heard the gunshot to check on you."

"What stopped you?"

"Whether you believe it or not, I can follow orders. I figured if someone killed you, my best chance was in here, and if you got the jump on one of them, you'd be back. I was going to give you another five minutes before reassessing what I needed to do. In the meantime, I checked the pockets of these two. No identification on them. All they brought with them was their Wilson Combat revolvers and this." She held her palm flat with a piece of paper on it. "A detailed map to this cabin."

"Great. They didn't just stumble upon us."

"You thought they did?"

"No, but I could dream they had and no one else knew about the cabin yet. At least until I could get you safely away from here."

Arianna's mouth pinched into a frown as she stared at the nearest dead assailant. "As you know, we have to assume the worse. Did the guy outside have anything on him?"

"He had a switchblade with blood on it and no ID."

Her gaze returned to his face. "No gun?"

"In a holster at the small of his back under his jacket. Not the best place to draw quickly. I surprised him coming around the corner. We're getting out of here."

"You're not calling this in?"

"No. Something isn't right. How did these guys find us? Where's Kevin?"

"Do you think he's dead, too, or that he let someone know I was here?"

"Don't know, and since I don't, I can't trust anyone until I know more. My job is to keep you alive to testify. I intend to do my job. Even more now. Rainwater has made this personal." Brody strode into the kitchen and washed the blood off his hands and face. "Get one of the marshals' duffel bags. Stuff what you think we can use in it. We don't have transport out of here, so we'll have to go on foot and find a place to camp. Bring food that is easy to carry. We won't use a fire to cook."

"Yeah, too risky."

He gestured at his bloody clothes. "I'm

changing and gathering what I can from the bedrooms. I imagine the ranger has a lot of what we may need for camping."

Arianna snapped her fingers. "Be right back." She rushed down the hallway and returned a half minute later with her camera.

"I don't think this is a good time to take pictures of the wilderness."

She smiled. "Not the wilderness but these two animals. When we get back to Anchorage, I want to make sure we find out who they are and who they work for."

"That's easy. Rainwater."

"But who they are might help us get Rainwater for a murder of a federal agent."

He covered the distance to the hall. "Are you sure you weren't a cop before this?"

"No, but when you protect others you learn things. Change and take care of those cuts or I will. There's a first aid kit in the bathroom."

"Don't have the time. I'll do it later. I want to leave in ten minutes. We don't know who else is out there and how long it will take them to realize these guys didn't succeed. When they figure that out, they'll come looking for us."

The thought there could be more than three sent to kill them spurred him to move as fast as his throbbing body allowed. Now that the adrenaline had faded, the pain came to the foreground. But he wouldn't allow it to interfere with what had to be done.

After snapping pictures of both of the intruders, Arianna found a backpack in the storage closet off the kitchen and decided to use that instead of one of the marshals' duffel bags. Easier to carry and since it was large it would hold about the same amount of items. As she stuffed what food she could into the bag, she glimpsed Mark on the floor nearby and steeled her resolve to bring to justice the person responsible for his death.

As a soldier she'd seen death, sometimes on a large scale. As a bodyguard she hadn't been exposed to it much in the past four years. She'd worked hard to keep it that way by protecting her clients the best she could. But now there were three dead bodies in the cabin and at least one outside, possibly Kevin's, too. She'd wanted to help and protect people without the death. But it had found her that evening when she'd witnessed Thomas Perkins's murder and wouldn't let go.

After scouring the kitchen and living room for anything they could use, she hurried to her bedroom and grabbed what she might need from her own possessions. The last things she put into her backpack were the camera and flashlight.

Although the night was only about four hours long, they might need the light, especially if they had to find shelter in a cave.

"Ready?" A rifle with a scope clutched in one hand and his duffel bag in the other, Brody stood in the entrance to her bedroom, dressed in clean jeans and T-shirt with hiking boots, a light parka and his Glock strapped in his holster at his waist. His face still looked as though the man had used him as a punching bag. When they were safely away from the cabin, she intended to treat those cuts.

She slung the pack onto her back. "Yes. Do we have all the ammunition?"

"Yes, what there is. I wish we had more rounds for the rifle, but for the handguns we should be fine. I found a map and a compass in the ranger's bedroom closet." He swung around and started for the front door.

Arianna followed. "I hate leaving Mark like this."

Brody stepped out onto the porch. "I can't call this in. I don't want anyone to know the assassins didn't succeed in killing us all. I don't know how they found us. I can't trust anyone."

"And we can't even take the satellite phone with us," she murmured, thinking about the GPS in cell phones. Great way to track someone.

"Not if we don't want more assassins finding us. We're on our own and I don't intend to make it easy for anyone to track us." Brody used the pair of binoculars hanging around his neck to scan the terrain stretching out before them.

"What happens when we reach Anchorage?"

"I'm not sure. I'll have to stash you someplace safe until you can testify because I intend to get you to that trial. Rainwater isn't going to win this one. One of my men, possibly two, are dead because of that man." He checked the compass then descended the steps. "Let's go."

"If they come after us, they'll know we're heading for Anchorage. There aren't too many ways in."

"I know. That's why we aren't going straight there. We're heading east toward Fairbanks, not southwest. They'll be watching all the direct routes to Anchorage."

"But we have to still get to Anchorage."

"Once I find some transportation, I'll figure out a way. I can't see us walking the whole way to Anchorage anyway. Time is against us. If they can't kill us, they'll still succeed in freeing Rainwater if you don't show up to testify."

"That isn't going to happen." She'd already waited so long for the chance to testify, spending almost two months in Kentucky until the U.S. Marshals Service had moved her back to Alaska. Two months separated from her family and friends. Her employer at Guardians, Inc. only knew that she had gone into the Witness Protection Program, and after that, she had to cut all ties. "I didn't go through the last two months for nothing." She ground her teeth, wishing she could grind her fists into the face of the person responsible for giving the cabin's location away.

"Even if you didn't get to testify, I doubt Rainwater would want you alive."

Arianna slanted a look at the harsh planes of Brody's face. Determination molded his features and steeled the hard look in his brown eyes. "That's my thinking, too. If I have to give up my life, I want it to be for something."

After Arianna took a picture of the third assailant, she and Brody headed toward the trees. The sun hung low on the horizon as it started its ascent. A dense stand of spruce, willow and birch up ahead offered them shelter from being in the open. Brody increased his pace the lighter the day became. When the thick wooded area swallowed them into a sea of green, he slowed his gait.

"If you need to rest, let me know. I tend to push."

"That's fine by me. But I do think we need to stop and take care of your cuts. Did the guy have a ring on?"

"You know at the time I didn't think about that. I was just trying to stop him."

"The cut over your eye is oozing blood. So is the one on your right cheek. Doesn't the scent of blood attract predators?"

"I guess it could. I didn't think about that, either. Too busy trying to figure out the best way to proceed. We'll stop for a brief rest after we've gone a little deeper into this forest."

"Maybe the U.S. Marshals Service will discover we're missing before the bad guys realize their assassin team didn't succeed."

A frown descended on Brody's beat-up face. "But who do we trust? I still can't figure out how they knew where we were. Few did. And the map that guy had was very precise."

"And another burning question is Kevin's whereabouts." Arianna pictured the young marshal with the ready smile. Did he betray them? What happened to him? Money lured a lot of people to do evil things. "I don't want them to find him dead, but what if he gave the cabin's location away? That was the first time he was on duty outside, and the assassins just happened to get inside the cabin without anyone knowing. They surprised Mark or we would have heard a commotion."

"That's what I'm wrestling with. I don't want to think it's one of us, but I have to consider that. Or—" Brody paused for a long moment "—it was someone from the first team at the cabin, especially because of the detailed map. Until we were flown in, I couldn't have drawn the kind of map they had. If it was Kevin, how could he have gotten the map to them ahead of time?"

"It has to have been an inside job, especially in light of the safe house being compromised in Anchorage. I don't believe in coincidences. Two places compromised in a case? Doesn't happen without inside information."

"And Rainwater has deep pockets. He's a crook but money can be influential."

As they went through a thicker area of trees, branches slapped against Arianna's arms while she threaded her way through the woods right behind Brody. "In a perfect world, money and power wouldn't count."

"It does in this world, and Rainwater has a lot of both. But somewhere along the line, we're going to have to trust someone, especially if we want to figure out who's behind this."

"I have to. My life will depend on that. I can't go into the Witness Protection Program with the thought that some marshal might have betrayed me and could do it again. Rainwater, even if he gets off, won't stop until I'm dead."

"Agreed." He halted and faced her, intensity

vibrating off him. "We have to discover who is behind this and get you to Anchorage to testify."

Blood trickled down his cheek. The urge to touch him and wipe it away assailed her. "This looks safe enough to stop for a few minutes. I need to take care of your cuts. You're still bleeding."

"A limb hit me in the face. Probably opened a few cuts that had clotted." Brody glanced around. "How about over there?"

"Fine." Arianna trekked to a less dense patch under a group of mountain alders. Dropping her pack on the ground, she relished the weight being off her shoulders for a few minutes. "Sit while I clean your cuts and bandage a couple of them." She retrieved the first aid kit and opened it.

"Did I tell you I'm not a good patient?"

"No, but too bad. I can't afford for you to get an infection."

"I doubt—" At that moment, she wiped the deepest cut on his cheek with a pad doused in alcohol, and he yanked back. "It's obvious you're no Florence Nightingale."

She grinned, winking at him. "Never claimed to be. I'm sure we shouldn't stay here long so speed is important." She moved on to the next wound.

"Yeah, the farther away we are from the cabin the safer we'll be."

He stayed perfectly still, his gaze fixed on her. She tried to ignore it, but it was hard. Her stomach clenched into a tight ball. His eyes seemed to penetrate deep into her—as though trying to discover her innermost secrets. She had no intention of sharing those with him or anyone.

"Close your eyes. I want to take care of the one near your left one. I wouldn't want to get alcohol in your eye."

His gaze narrowed for a few seconds before he shut it completely. She dabbed the pad on the cut, relieved for the short break from his intense look. Slowly the knots unraveled in her gut. With his eyes closed, she got a chance to scrutinize him without him seeing. His features weren't handsome, but there was a strength and ruggedness to them that gave a person the impression he knew how to take care of himself. That appealed to her. Probably too much.

Caring about a person who was protecting you wasn't wise. Just as caring about a person you were protecting wasn't wise. Her hand quivered as she pressed a small bandage over the cut near his eye, then proceeded to put two more on the other ones that kept bleeding.

"What made you go into the private sector as a bodyguard?"

His question surprised her, and yet it shouldn't

have. He no doubt was assessing her and deciding if he could trust her to protect his back. Whether he liked it or not, they were in this as a team. "Instead of law enforcement?"

"Yes."

"Money and the freedom my job allows me. When I left the service, I knew I wanted to use my skills to protect people. In my different tours in the army, I saw a lot of defenseless people who were victims of their circumstances. Guardians, Inc. is a business but Kyra Hunt, my boss, also helps people who can't usually afford to have a paid bodyguard."

"When I knew I would be protecting you, I did some checking into Guardians, Inc. It's a top-notch company with a good reputation."

"Kyra only employs the best."

"And she hired you?"

She laughed. "I'll try not to be offended by that remark."

"Don't be. I've read about your assignments. You're very good at your job."

Ignoring his remark, she taped the last bandage into place. "I'm finished. You're not as good as new, but it will have to do." She put the packaging from the items she'd used back into the first aid kit, not wanting to leave any evidence they had been there behind for someone to find.

His eyes remained closed.

"You didn't fall asleep on me, did you?"

"No, I was running through my mind what went down at the cabin, trying to figure out what happened, how they might have known where we were. How did they get there? Who would have talked with them?"

"Any clues?"

His eyelids slowly rose, and his look snared hers. "No, and now we don't have the time to dally and try to figure it out. Let's go." He pushed to his feet.

Arianna stood, stretching to ease the tightness in her shoulders and back. "I'm ready." She reached for her pack when a roar echoed through the stand of trees. A familiar roar.

She shot up and whirled around. Through the woods a large grizzly bear standing on its hind legs stared right at them.

THREE

Forty yards separated Arianna from the grizzly, still perched on its hind legs. Watching. "Is this the same one that was at the cabin?"

"Don't know. I don't see any cubs around."

"Oh, good. *Another* bear. What do we do? Run? Climb the tree behind us?"

Brody turned his head slightly but still kept tabs on the brown bear by slanting a glance toward it. "Don't look directly at it."

"But—"

Before she could finish her sentence Brody straightened as tall as he could, raised his arms and waved them. "Bears are curious. I'm challenging it. Follow suit." Then in a shout he said, "Leave us alone," over and over.

Arianna mimicked what Brody was doing, hoping he knew what he was doing. She was all for spinning around and running as fast as her legs could carry her.

The grizzly dropped to all four legs. It charged them but stopped about twenty-five yards away.

"This isn't working." Arianna's heartbeat sped, her mouth dry. She might not have to worry about Rainwater's men.

"Back away slowly, still waving your arms and shouting."

"Isn't this calling attention to us?"

"Yep, but a gunshot would make more noise. Carry farther."

One step back. Then another. Arianna looked sideways at the bear. It stood on its hind legs again, pointing its nose up in the air as though the grizzly was sniffing it. She kept moving, going between two trees.

"Are you sure we shouldn't climb a tree?"

"Grizzly bears can climb a tree."

"What else can they do?" Arianna asked, watching the animal lower itself onto all fours again.

"Swim and run fast."

The bear roared.

Arianna gasped while Brody brought the rifle up.

The grizzly gave one last vocal protest then loped off toward the east, disappearing in the thickness of a stand of pines.

Brody rotated around. "Let's get out of here before it changes its mind and returns for us."

"Now you're talking." But as she hurried away, she glanced back every few steps to make sure the bear wasn't behind them. The pounding of her pulse echoed through her mind.

"We need to keep moving. It's been several hours since we were attacked. If I was running that mission, I'd be wondering why my men hadn't come back and go investigate."

"The Marshals Service will investigate when you don't call in this morning."

"Yes, so the best thing for us is to put as much distance between us and the cabin. We don't want anyone to know where we are, not even the marshals. When we get to Fairbanks, we can check the news to see what, if anything, is being said."

Arianna slowed her pace and twisted around once more to make sure the bear wasn't following them. She'd heard stories about a bear tracking a person, appearing every once in a while then attacking. She didn't want to be one of those stories. All she saw was a thick, green forest around her—a perfect place for someone—or some animal—to hide and wait for the right time to strike.

After a couple of hours of walking as fast as they could through dense woods and rugged terrain, Brody spied a place that probably had been used as a campsite in the past. Thankfully it showed no signs of recent use. "Let's stop and eat something." He pointed at a crop of rocks. "I'm going up there to scout out our surroundings." He took out his compass. "And make sure we're going in the right direction."

"Did I tell you I don't cook?" Arianna said with a laugh. "So all you'll get is something easy. Like peanut butter sandwiches without the jelly, and I'm afraid the bread has been squashed."

After finding his first foothold, Brody peered at Arianna already digging into her backpack. "Right now anything sounds good. I'm starving."

"So am I."

Her gaze linked with his, and he glimpsed the toll the past hours had taken on Arianna. There were many people he guarded in the Witness Protection Program, but some were criminals. The ones like Arianna always got to him. The ones who weren't trying to cut a deal or avoid the consequences of their actions, but were simply testifying because it was the right thing to do, no matter what the cost. He couldn't imagine giving up his life and having to start a new one. But she would have to once the trial was over.

He climbed the outcropping of rocks until he reached a perch where he could lie down and scope out the area without being seen. He was most concerned with the terrain between them and the cabin.

The wind whipped against his face, carrying the scent of burning wood. A campfire nearby? Frowning, he focused the binoculars in the direction they'd come. A roiling mushroom of dark smoke billowed into the sky.

Was the cabin burning? The forest around it?

He trained his binoculars on the area, trying to see anything that would give him an idea of what they were up against. He couldn't tell. After checking all the surroundings, he scrambled down the rocks and hurried to Arianna.

"We need to keep moving."

She handed him a sandwich. "Take a few minutes to eat." Studying his face, she pushed to her feet. "What's wrong?"

"There's a fire behind us and the wind is blowing this way. I'm guessing it's four miles back, but it has been dry in this part of Alaska, so there's a lot of dry timber between us and the forest fire." He took a bite of the sandwich, hefted his duffel bag and then slung his rifle over his shoulder. "Let's go. We'll eat and walk."

"You think Rainwater's men started a fire at the cabin? Why would they do that?"

"Maybe to cover up any evidence. To cause confusion. They had to know the U.S. Marshals

Service would know when something happened at the cabin."

"The fire means a lot of firefighters will be in this area."

"Making it harder for us. Rainwater's men can infiltrate the firefighters, using that as a cover for being here."

Arianna nodded as she finished the last of her sandwich. "Which way?"

"There's a river up ahead of us." He checked the compass then pointed northeast. "We'll have to cross it. It should be low because of no rainfall in the past month, but we'll still have to swim."

Arianna slowed her gait. "Is there a way around the river?"

"It stands between us and Fairbanks. Why?"

"I can't swim well. Just enough to get by."

"You can't?" He'd never considered that. "Why not?"

"I almost drowned as a child. I was caught in a flood. Rushing water scares me. Is this river like that?"

"Yes. At least when it's low you can see the rocks." He wished there was another way to get across other than swimming. Arianna had already gone through enough.

She stopped and swept around toward him. The pallor on her face highlighted her fear. "I can do a lot of things. Climb up tall structures. Parachute out of a plane. Snakes, rats, spiders don't bother me, but rushing water does. I'm only okay in a pool—still water."

He hated to see the fear in her eyes, but there was nothing he could say to make it better. "We don't have the time to find a way around the river. We have to cross it and there isn't a bridge for miles. Besides, those will be watched."

Closing her eyes, she drew in a deep breath. "Okay."

She rotated back around and started forward, her strides long. But Brody had glimpsed how scared she was and wasn't sure how they would get across the river that was a favorite of those who liked to ride the rapids.

Brody came down from climbing a tree to check the progress of the fire. His grim expression spoke of their dire situation even before he said, "It's moving fast. Faster than us. Animals are fleeing the area—an elk herd is off to the right of us. But what is even more alarming is that I saw three dogs with several handlers—all armed. No uniforms on so we need to assume unfriendly."

Dogs. Tracking dogs were hard to evade. Determined and relentless described the ones she'd worked with in the past in the service. "We're boxed in then with the river on one side and the fire and dogs on the other."

"Yes, and they are about two miles ahead of the fire so let's getting moving."

Arianna thrust a bottle of water into his hand. "Drink, and eat this protein bar. We're gonna need to keep our energy up."

After taking a swig of water, he started out at a fast clip, making his own path through the forest. "We've got to eat on the run. No other way."

As she set into a jog, Arianna wolfed down her food. Her muscles burned from exhaustion and only her strong determination kept her putting one foot in front of the other. She refused to dwell on what she would face at the river. The scent of the fire intensified even as they moved away from it. When she inhaled deep breaths as she ran, she couldn't fill her lungs with enough oxygen. Pain in her side stabbed her, her breathing grew more labored with each stride she took.

She periodically looked over her shoulder, checking the area behind her. At any second she had to be prepared to encounter people. Whether friend or foe didn't matter because they couldn't take a chance on being seen.

Brody came to an abrupt halt, his arm going up to indicate he heard something ahead of them. Arianna nearly collided with him but managed to stop in time.

He pointed to the left then whispered into her ear, "Someone's coming."

Arianna glimpsed something orange where he'd indicated. She scanned the forest, saw a place they could hide and tugged on Brody. She just hoped it wasn't a tracker with a dog or their hiding would be in vain.

As quiet as possible, she crept through the underbrush with Brody at her side. Lying down on the forest floor beneath some dense foliage, she pulled her gun, praying she didn't have to use it. Brody brought the rifle around and aimed it in the direction where he saw the orange.

Two men dressed as hunters, rifles in their hands, trekked *toward* the fire. While in Kentucky, Arianna had familiarized herself with every person known to be associated with Joseph Rainwater. She had planned on going back to Alaska as prepared as she could be. The larger of the two that passed within ten yards of their location was Boris Mankiller, an appropriate name for him because he was believed to be one of Rainwater's most valuable guns for hire.

Mankiller and his comrade halted about twenty feet away. Mankiller made a slow circle, his rifle raised as though he sensed them nearby. Her heartbeat hammered so fast and loud she wondered if he heard it.

Brody signaled he had his rifle pointed at Mankiller. She lifted her Glock and targeted the man's comrade, her breath bottled in her lungs.

One minute passed. Mankiller pointed at the sky in the direction of the fire. Arianna glimpsed the growing smoke, obscuring the sun and leaving a dimness in the forest as if it were dusk instead of the middle of the day.

The two parted—one went to the left while the other moved to the right and slightly toward the fire, fanning out. She saw through the foliage another pair of guys a hundred yards away. She leaned toward Brody and whispered, "They're trying to close in on us."

"They may be part of an inner ring around the cabin. We need to watch for any people forming an outer circle. Let's go. It's even more important to get to the river."

When he said the word *river,* a ripple of fear snaked down her spine but her fear of the water was far outweighed by fear of the men after her. In this small part of the forest she knew that Rainwater had four men looking for them. Multiply that over the large area of this wilderness and he must have hired a small army to look for her and anyone left to protect her.

Sneaking out from under the brush, she ran

while crouched right behind Brody, swinging her attention back every once in a while to make sure no one had spotted them. Her back hurt from being hunched over and her thighs screamed in protest at the punishing pace Brody set but she didn't dare voice a complaint.

Forty-five minutes later, Arianna stared down at the raging river, its water churning like a boiling pot of liquid. She froze at the sight.

Brody came up beside her. "You okay?"

She opened her mouth to answer him, but no words formed in her mind, her full attention glued to river. Reminders of when she had been young and swept away from her parents in something similar inundated her. Her younger sister had died in the flood. Arianna had tried to save her, but her grip on Lily had slipped away. The last thing she remembered was her sister's scream reverberating through her head against the backdrop of the gushing sound of the water—a raging turmoil.

Brody grasped her arm and swung her around. He waited until her gaze latched on to his before saying, "All you have to do is get yourself across the river. I'll take care of everything else. Okay?"

She nodded, her mouth so dry she should be happy to immerse herself in water. She wasn't.

Fear held her immobile, unable to take a step toward the bank.

She hadn't known how hard controlling her fear had been until her army unit had been forced to cross a swollen river. Watching one of her comrades swept away by the power of the water brought her childhood trauma to the forefront after years buried deep in her subconscious.

"We don't have much time to get across the river and hide before the dogs track us to here."

Her attention drifted away from the water to focus on Brody. "What do you need me to do?"

"We need to wade in the water along the edge as far upstream as we can go, then go straight across. They'll assume the current will take us downstream."

"Or they might assume the opposite. Either way we'll be taking a chance. Actually with all the men I have a feeling are out here, they probably can cover both areas."

"Don't forget they can't be openly looking for you. By now the U.S. Marshals Service is all over here, too."

"If only we knew who to trust."

"Can't take the chance. You don't know how much that pains me to say."

She stared into his brown eyes, full of sadness. "I was betrayed by a team member, so yes, I do know how you feel."

"When we have time, you'll have to tell me about that." He took her hand and started down the incline to the river.

Scaring off a bear was nothing to Arianna, but this was a big deal. She stepped into the water until it was swirling about her ankles. Still grasping her hand, Brody led her a few more feet out to where the river came up to her knees, then he trudged upstream. The feel of his fingers around her fortified her with the knowledge she wasn't alone to face her worst fear.

After about a hundred feet up the river, Brody rounded a corner and came face to face with the water racing over a mound of rocks. Blocked from going any farther in the shallow part of the river, he stopped and took her backpack. He opened it and gave it to Arianna to hold.

"You can't swim holding the rifle and a duffel bag," she said.

After removing some rope from his duffel bag, he piled it into the backpack then began adding other items. "I know. I'm putting what I think we need the most in the backpack. The rest I'll sink in the middle of these rocks. It'll be hard to find."

He left food or items that would be ruined from being dunked in the river in the duffel bag, then scrambled up the rocks. When he slipped and fell back into the river, Arianna rushed to help him. Suddenly she realized she stood in thigh-deep water with a strong current tugging at her. Panic seized her. She shoved it down. She had no time to be afraid. The alternative was to stay on this side of the river and try to evade tracking dogs and men with rifles.

She waded to Brody and helped him up, taking the backpack from his hand. "I'll toss you it when you get up on top of the rocks."

This time he succeeded without the burden of carrying the pack. She threw it to him. He caught it and disappeared from view. Arianna hastened back closer to shore and waited. Two minutes passed and worry nipped at her composure. She thought about shouting his name over the rushing sound of the water, but that might only lead the dogs and men to their location.

Opening and closing her hands, she gritted her teeth. She'd never been good at waiting. *Lord, I know I haven't been talking with You lately, but please help Brody and me get to Anchorage safely. Rainwater needs to go to prison for what he did. I need You.*

The last sentence had been the hardest to say because she'd come to depend on herself so much in the past four years. *I don't know if I can make it across this river without Your help.*

As she stared at the rushing river, the earlier tension eased. Suddenly Brody popped up over the rocks then lowered himself down into the water.

He sloshed to her and took the rope and backpack. He slung the backpack over his shoulders, then lifted the rope. "I'm tying this around your chest. This'll be your line to use. As long as you're attached, I should be able to help you. Don't go in until I reach the other side."

He moved farther out into the rapids, water hitting the rocks and spraying up into the air. With long, even strokes, he headed for the opposite bank at an angle. He didn't stop until he was over on the other shore. Waving to her, he held up the rope and signaled for her to start.

Sucking in a steadying breath that did nothing to fill her lungs, she waded as far as she could, fighting to keep herself upright with the strong current. Even though Brody had swam at an angle upstream, he'd ended up about ten feet downstream. Was that far enough away from where they first went into the river? But even more importantly, could she keep herself from being swept up in the current?

Two seconds later she plunged into the river, using all the strength she had to dog-paddle toward the other side. Water splashed over her head, and she went under, swallowing some of the river water. Panic threatened to take over. Again she fought to squash it as she struggled to the surface. Her head came up out of the water, and she gasped for air at the same time the current slammed her against some rocks. Black swirled before her eyes.

FOUR

Brody saw Arianna go under halfway across the river, and his first impulse was to drop the rope and go into the water after her. Instead, he searched for something to tie the rope to then he'd go after her, using it to guide him to her. He used a tree nearby, keeping his eye on the area where she went under.

As he hurried into the river, she surfaced feet from some large boulders. Before he could do anything, she crashed into the rocks like a wet rag doll. Next the river swept her limp body, bobbing up and down, into the fast current, heading away from him.

The rope grew taut, the thin tree he'd tied it to bowing but holding strong for the time being. Gripping the line, he held on to it and swam the fastest he could with one arm. The rush of the river tossed him about and drenched him as he tried to get to Arianna.

Then the churning water swamped him, pushing him under, and he lost sight of Arianna.

Pain jerked Arianna from the black void. For a second she didn't know where she was until the same feeling of drowning from when she was child overwhelmed all her senses. Her chest felt as though it were about to explode. She needed to breathe. She couldn't. Water encased her like a tomb. She couldn't see through the murkiness as she tossed and twisted in the river.

I can't panic.

Lord, help.

A memory punched through the panic. Brody had tied a rope around her. A lifeline. She fumbled for it, her fingers grazing the rope about her torso. When she grasped the length connected to Brody, she willed what strength she had left into her arms and pulled. One hand over the other. Again. And again.

Light filtered through the dim water. The surface. Air. She moved quicker while her lungs burned in excruciating pain.

I won't—let—Rain—

She broke free of her watery tomb. Oxygen-rich air flooded her starved lungs. Her thinking sharpened. That was when she realized her grip on the rope started slipping. She clutched it and began dragging herself toward shore. Her gaze latched on to Brody only a few yards from her in the river. Although still tossed about, she fixed her full attention on him as he came closer.

When she reached him, he enclosed an arm around her, a smile on his face—the most beautiful thing she'd seen in a long time.

He treaded water. "Okay?"

She nodded.

"Hold on to the rope. I'll be next to you."

Those words made her feel totally taken care of and protected. Something she did for people, not the other way around. The calmness that descended surprised her because they still had half the river to cross. Was this what she instilled in her clients—this sense of security? Then she remembered in her time of need calling out to the Lord. That was when she was able to calm herself and get to the surface.

When she pushed to her feet a couple of yards from the bank, her shaky legs barely held her upright. Brody slung his arm around her and helped her to shore. She collapsed on the ground, still inhaling gulps of air as though she couldn't get enough of it, like a person left in a desert without water.

Hovering over her, he offered her his hand. "I wish I could give you a minute to rest, but we can't stay here. No doubt the men and dogs will end up at this river soon. We've got to keep moving."

"I know." She fit her hand in his, and he tugged her to her feet. "And you don't have to worry about me. I know what has to be done."

He grinned, untying the rope from the tree and reeling the long length in. "I'd like all my witnesses to cooperate like this. Maybe I can hire you to teach them."

"Sure, but I think that would be breaking a number of WitSec rules," she said, using the shortened nickname for Witness Security.

"Yeah, I guess I'll still have to keep trying to train my witnesses myself." Brody picked up the backpack and slung it over his shoulders, then reached for the rifle.

"Let me carry something."

"Let me play the male here and take both."

"Can't give up that gun? Now that doesn't surprise me. But I can take the backpack at least part of the way."

Brody gave it to her, then climbed up the bank of the river.

Arianna tried clambering up the incline behind him and nearly slid back down. She gripped a small tree growing out of the mini cliff and kept herself stationary. The swim had taken more out of her than she realized. "Okay. You can have the backpack for now."

Standing above her on the rise, he bent over and grasped one arm then hoisted her up. "When we get away from the river, we'll stop and eat something while I take care of your injuries."

Finally, at the top of a small ridge, Arianna glanced down at herself. Cuts and marks that would probably become bruises later covered her arms. She hoped the jeans protected her legs or she'd look like she'd been through a meat grinder. She touched her face and winced. When she peered at her hand, blood was smeared on her fingertips.

As they progressed across a clearing toward the forest at the bottom of a mountain range, her body protested each step she took. Everything had happened so fast in the river, but she must have been knocked against the rocks pretty hard to feel this bad.

An hour later at the bottom of a mountain beneath a line of trees, Arianna sat at the base of an aspen and leaned back against its whitish trunk. "This isn't gonna be easy to go over."

"No, but this range goes for miles. Walking around isn't an option with the clock on the trial ticking down."

"Not a complaint. An observation. With the right equipment I love to climb mountains."

"Sorry, all we have is rope, and I'm not sure

how good that will be for us." Brody took out the first aid kit. "Let's get you patched up. Your cuts aren't bleeding anymore, but I'd feel better if they are cleaned. I remember a wise woman telling me that cuts can get infected."

With Brody only a half a foot from her, she wished she had a mirror in all the items she'd thought to bring. His nearness did strange things to her inside. As he looked into her face, the chocolate brown of his eyes mesmerized her, holding her tethered to him without the use of any ropes. His touch as he tended to her injuries was gentle, in direct contradiction of his muscular, male physique. Through the sting of alcohol, she concentrated on him.

"I don't know much about you personally, and since I didn't have the advantage of reading up on you before you came to the cabin, maybe you could tell me a little about yourself."

His hand stilled; his gaze locked with hers. "What do you want to know?"

"Are you married?" came out before Arianna had time to censor her question. Although she really wanted to know, she could have phrased it a little less obviously. "I mean you aren't wearing a wedding ring, but some men don't. Is there a wife waiting for you to come home? Children? I mean not that it's important…" She clenched her teeth together to keep from making it worse by explaining why she'd asked. That was when she realized how dangerous his touch, his nearness was. She forced herself to look at a point behind him.

"I have no one to worry that I won't be home. This job requires a lot of time away from my home, not to mention putting my life on the line to protect a witness. I won't subject a wife to that kind of uncertainty."

"That was the way I felt about my job, first in the army and then with Guardians, Inc. I was usually gone from my home three weeks out of four, sometimes more. Not easy to have a relationship that way."

"Sounds like our lives are similar."

"Not exactly, at least now. My bodyguarding days were over when I became the star witness against Joseph Rainwater."

"I'm sorry about that." He took out a pair of scissors. "I want to cut the sleeves off your shirt. They're shredded anyway."

She glanced at the ruined shirt and nodded. "When I get a chance, I'll be chucking it. Not a souvenir I want to keep of this trip."

His laughter filled the air. "True."

Arianna looked away from him again before she forgot how serious their situation was.

"It's my turn to ask you a question. Why did

you leave the army? From what I read about your service record, you were very good at your job."

"Being in the army had been in my blood since I was a child. My father served in the army as do two of my brothers. A third brother is a Navy SEAL, and my family hasn't let him forget it. I'd planned to stay in."

"What changed your mind?" Brody cleaned each scrape and cut on her right arm, his fingers whispering across her skin.

Goose bumps rose on her flesh. She knew he saw them and wished she could control her reaction to his touch and proximity. "The army didn't appeal to me anymore." She couldn't share what had happened to her. It was too personal. The team member's betrayal still cut deep.

"How did your family feel about your decision?"

"Hey, I believe—" she twisted toward him "—it's my turn to ask a question."

"I can't get anything by you," he said with a contrite look.

She chuckled. "I may be exhausted, but I'm still sharp up here," she said and tapped her temple. "What made you become a U.S. marshal?"

"Probably the same reason you became a bodyguard. To protect those needing to be protected. I had a friend in school who was bullied by a group of boys. I found myself standing up to them and liking the feeling of protecting Aaron. I hated seeing what those kids were doing to him. He didn't want to go to school. He stayed in his house. It changed him."

"But you often guard criminals that have agreed to testify for a lesser sentence or protection in the program. They're not exactly innocent."

"Yes, but their testimony gets some criminals convicted that are often untouchable without their testimony. Besides, if those criminals weren't protected, they would be killed for daring to testify against the people running things. Everyone should be able to do what is right, to start over in life." He put the antiseptic swabs he didn't use back into the first aid kit. The ones he'd used, he stuck in the backpack pocket where trash went. Nothing was left behind to be found by the people after them.

"I've discovered everything isn't black-and-white," Arianna said. "There's a whole lot of gray in life."

"That's a good way to put it." After withdrawing another protein bar, he gave it to her. "This isn't much, but we really shouldn't take any more time to rest. Let's get over this mountain first."

As Arianna looked up the slope, thousands

of feet high, the scent from the blaze on the other side of the river invaded her surroundings. Through the break in the tree canopy, she caught glimpses of the haze caused by the fire. "Yeah, we need to get over by nightfall."

"What nightfall?"

"I know it's not much, but it does get dark for a few hours. I've had to come down a mountain in the night. Not fun."

"Maybe there's somewhere we can rest up there. Find a place where we can see if anyone is coming up this side."

Arianna moved until she found a large hole in the canopy and shielded her eyes from the sunlight. "There doesn't look like there's one, but maybe there's a cave tucked in up there for us."

Several thousand feet higher than the surrounding forest, Brody situated himself between two boulders, lying flat on the ground and looking upon the terrain below. Using the binoculars, he scoped out the area between the mountain and the river.

Activity across the river near where they had come out of the woods caught his full attention. They were too far away to see if it was Mankiller, but there were three men and two dogs. Not good. And where was the other dog he'd seen earlier?

Still, they might be able to rest and sleep for a couple of hours. He hoped the men chasing them were smart enough not to try to climb the mountain in the dark. Arianna and he had had a hard time doing it in daylight.

Arianna crawled up next to him. "Anything?"

He passed her the binoculars. "What do you think we should do? Stay and rest a little or keep going?" She was in good condition. From Ted's daily reports he knew she worked out each morning, keeping in shape. Even after that battering she took in the rapids, she still wouldn't stop.

She turned toward him, one eyebrow raised. "You're asking my opinion?"

"Yes. You're part of this two-person team. If you can't make it, then there's no reason for us to try to hurry down the other side."

"Even if I was dead on my feet, there's no way I would pass up a challenge like that. I can make it down the mountain. We have enough rope to do the Dulfersitz rappel method. It was what climbers used in the 1800s before all the safety equipment we use today was created. It works, especially in this situation. Rappelling is a faster way down the other side of the mountain. It's dangerous, but the alternative is even more dangerous."

"Yeah, Rainwater's men are catching up with us."

"We'll have to leave the rope dangling from the mountain because we'll have to tie it to an anchor up here."

He peered at the three men and dogs across the river. "We have no choice. I've never rappelled, but I've done some rock climbing on indoor walls."

"You're in good hands. I've done it a lot."

She'd trusted him that he would get her across the river. He would trust her this once to get him down the mountain rappelling, but beyond that he couldn't totally put his trust in anyone. He crawled back away from the edge and stood when the rocks behind him gave him cover from the men after them. "I'm game. If you can swim across a raging river, I can go down the mountain the fast way."

"Not the fastest. That way would kill you." She grabbed the rope and searched her surroundings. She made her way to a rock jutting up and tested it to see if it was firmly in place. "I'll anchor the rope to this." After tying the rope to the boulder, she knotted the ends of the rope. "I wouldn't want you to rappel off the end of it."

"Thanks. I wouldn't want to either. You think it will reach all the way?"

"Let's see." She went to the edge and dropped it over. "It's about a hundred feet to the ledge. The rope almost reaches it. We'll have to drop the last yard, but it looks pretty flat and there's enough room. The rest of the way looks easier—probably like what you did at the indoor rock wall?"

"I know I don't take the rope and hand over hand creep down it."

"No. I'll show you how you need to do it, then I want you to try. You'll go first." Arianna put the rope between her legs then brought it around her front, across her torso and over her left shoulder. She held the rope anchored to the boulder in her left hand and the other end of it in her right one, behind her and near her waist. "This will help you control your descent. Do you think you can do it?"

"There's only one way to find out." When she stepped away and gave him the rope, he took it and mimicked her earlier position.

"Good. Now when you lower yourself over the ledge, you're going to walk yourself down the side of the mountain. Slow and steady. When you get down there, I will lower the backpack and rifle to you, then follow after that. Okay?"

"I don't like leaving you up here by yourself."

"No choice. Besides, I can—"

"Take care of yourself. I know. I've seen you in action. Even in the river you didn't give up."

"Giving up isn't an option. I told you I'm not gonna let Rainwater win. I saw what he did to Esther's husband and most likely he's responsible for doing something to Esther." Her voice roughened as she finished her sentence.

His respect for her went up another notch. She continually amazed him. In all the witnesses he'd protected, he'd never encountered someone quite like her. "Let's do this."

He walked backward to the edge of the cliff, paused and looked at her, her long white-blond hair pulled up in a ponytail. The wind played with it, causing strands to dance about her shoulders. Her eyes appeared silver in the light.

Easing himself over the ledge, he let the rope slide slowly in his grasp. His heart rate spiked as he began walking down the almost ninety-degree rock facade. He peered up at Arianna watching him, worry apparent in those silver-gray eyes.

He forced a smile of reassurance to his lips although that was the last thing he felt. "I'm fine."

"You're doing great. Are you sure you haven't done this before?"

"Yep. I think I'd remember it," he said, his hands burning from the scrape of twine across his palms. No wonder climbers used gloves. Too bad they didn't have any.

An eternity later he came to the end of the rope, and finally looked down at where he was. Three feet to the wide ledge. With a deep breath, he pushed out of the makeshift harness slightly and dropped. When his feet landed on the stone surface, he bent down, absorbing the impact from the ground with his legs.

Immediately he straightened and shouted, "Piece of cake. I've got a new hobby when we get out of this. Send the backpack and rifle down."

"Coming." Arianna raised the rope, tied the objects on it then lowered them to him.

Not long after that, she started rappelling down the side of the mountain. What took him ten minutes she did in seven. He wished when this was over that they could rappel together with the proper equipment, especially gloves. But after she testified, she would leave Alaska for a new home, in an undisclosed place. With her location compromised, she wouldn't return to where she had been before coming to Alaska to testify. Whoever was behind the cabin attack might have discovered her previous residence.

When she planted her feet on the ledge, he finally breathed normally. Although she knew what she was doing rappelling, their equipment wasn't something most climbers would use and the sport was dangerous, even in desirable conditions. These were less than advantageous. Desperate was a better description.

He inched toward the edge to stare down at the rest of their descent to the base of the mountain. "Once we are about halfway, we should be able to walk. It might be a steep one, but we won't have to climb down."

The stone shelf ran about fifty feet across. Arianna moved down its length and stopped not far from one end. "Let's go down here. It isn't the easiest way, but it slopes into a different area from where you're standing so if they find the rope and bring dogs in from below this will give us more time."

He approached her and peered around her. The angle was seventy or eighty degrees, which wasn't much better than what they had done, but a lot of rocks jutted out to use as steps. "Agreed."

"We'll go together. There's room for us both to descend near each other. I'm carrying the backpack. You can sling the rifle over your shoulder."

"You can tell you like to be in charge."

"In this case it's only because I've done this probably a lot more than you. Balance is important and the backpack might throw you off.

Doing this in an indoor place is different from outside with the elements."

"I bow to your superior experience." He bent forward at the waist and swept his arm out.

She chuckled. "It's nice we have different skill sets or no telling what kind of trouble we would be in by now."

He turned in a full circle. "It'll be dark in an hour and a half."

Arianna took the backpack and shrugged into it. "The bottom part of the mountain will be a cinch after this."

Twenty minutes later Brody hung in the middle of the rock wall, Arianna about a yard from him, below him slightly. The skill she exhibited marveled him. Too bad this wasn't the time or place to admire them. He couldn't lose his focus on protecting her. Admiring her would have to wait. She'd slowed her descent because of him.

His left hand grasped onto a hold, and then he found a rock outcropping for his right one. Next, he lowered himself until he found a foothold that would take his weight and brought his left foot to it. When he shifted to place his right foot on a one-inch ledge, he began looking for his next move.

"Doing okay?" Arianna called up to him.

"Yes." He leaned toward the left, reaching for an indentation in the rock facade.

His right foot slipped off the foothold, plunging into the air.

FIVE

Arianna looked up to check on Brody's progress, and was just in time to see the ledge where his right foot gave way. For a second his leg hung in midair. He floundered, teetering for a second, before he finally lost his balance and plummeted.

When his body hit against a small stone ledge, the rifle shimmied down his flapping arms and dropped to the ground below. He clasped the rock shelf, breaking his downward fall.

Arianna swallowed a scream and moved as fast as she could to get to him. He hung under the protrusion, trying to secure his hold. In the midst of rushing, she lost her grip but hadn't moved her feet yet. She searched for another hold and dug in, determined to get to him before he lost his grasp. His legs flailed as he searched for a place to put his feet.

She was capable, but she didn't want to do

this alone. She needed help. *Please, God, keep him safe.*

She probably wouldn't have made it across the river without him. She wasn't going to let him die. Feeling utterly helpless at the moment, she mumbled over and over a prayer of protection for Brody.

When she was a couple of feet from him, she saw his arms begin to slip from around the stone outcropping. She lunged toward it with her right foot as his grasp first on the left then the right came loose. Recklessly she leaped totally onto the small ledge and went down to grip him. Her fingers grabbed air.

All she could do was watch Brody crash downward the remaining few yards. As he lay collapsed, completely still at the bottom, Arianna hurried her descent.

Please, please let him be alive.

A constriction about her chest squeezed tighter the closer she came to him. She jumped down the last feet and shrugged off the backpack as she knelt next to him. With a quivering hand, she felt for his pulse at his neck. It beat beneath her fingertips, and relief shivered down her.

A second later, the sweetest thing she'd heard was his groan. Then he moved.

"Take it easy. Where do you hurt?"

Carefully he rolled over and looked up into her face. "Everywhere."

"That doesn't surprise me. You had quite a fall. That's why you don't climb without ropes and safety gear."

One corner of his mouth quirked up. "Thanks for telling me now. You could work on your timing."

"I do believe you're gonna be all right if your comebacks are any indication."

"What about my head? It's throbbing."

She probed his scalp, producing an "ouch" from him. "You might have a concussion. You've got a nasty gash to go with all the new scrapes you acquired on your plunge downward. Don't you remember I said it might be the fastest way down but not the safest?"

"I'll keep that in mind next time. Wait, there isn't going to be a next time. I don't think rock climbing and me go together," he said as he struggled to his elbows, flinching as he planted them on the ground to prop himself up. "At least the ground isn't tilting too much."

"Tilting? It's flat right here."

"Oh, then things may be worse than I thought." As he pushed himself to a sitting position, he closed his eyes.

"Is your world spinning?"

"In slo-mo, but yes, it's spinning."

"Then we aren't going anywhere for the time being."

"We can't stay here. We need to get the rest of the way down the mountain."

Arianna peered up at the dimming sky—some of the darkness from the sun going down, some from the smoke of the fire. "Not in the dark. It's bad enough navigating over rough terrain when you are in top physical condition, but when you're suffering probably from a concussion, no." She emphasized that last word.

"Did anyone ever tell you that you're bossy?"

"A few clients have, but they usually came to appreciate it in the end."

Putting his palms on the rocky earth beside him, he shoved himself up and immediately crumpled back onto the ground. "Okay, we'll stay here and have something to eat, rest a little bit but not long. I'm leaving in an hour and you're coming with me."

"I could argue with you."

"You could, but I'm an injured man. Surely you wouldn't add any more distress to me than a fall from twenty feet up a side of a rocky mountain."

"Oh, please, don't pull the woe-is-me card."

He eased back onto the ground and closed his eyes. "I'll just rest for a few minutes."

The comment was said casually but with a thread of pain that heightened her worry. "You going to sleep?"

"No, just trying to alleviate some of the tap dancers in my head. They're having a jolly ole time at my expense."

Arianna brought the backpack around and rummaged inside until she found the first aid kit at the bottom. When she opened it, she saw that some of the contents were ruined from the swim in the river, but the pain relievers in the packets weren't. She shook out two tablets and opened a new bottle of water. "Here, take these. They might help."

Lifting his head, he grimaced. He took the pills and swallowed a mouthful of liquid. "I've got a feeling this is like throwing a pail of water on a raging fire." He settled back on the ground. "Do I look as bad as I feel?"

Her gaze trekked down his length. His torn shirt matched hers after her encounter with the rapids and his scrapes against the rocks left welts and abrasions all over him. "I never thought you were the kind of guy who worried about his good looks."

He opened one eye. "I have good looks?"

"I'm not answering that question. It might swell your head even more."

He smiled. "You're not half-bad either."

"I'm warning you now. I'm cleaning as many of your scrapes as I can with the limited first aid kit we have. I think we have almost exhausted its contents. We seem to be accident-prone."

"And the river...didn't help...either. I'm glad you..." His voice faded the more he spoke until no words came out.

She felt his pulse again. Strong. That reassured her. About all she could do was pour antiseptic on the worst of the wounds. There was no gauze left that wasn't wet with river water. They needed to find somewhere she could really tend to his new injuries. When they reached civilization she was going to insist on trying to find some kind of help.

As she finished what she could do with the antiseptic, she sat back and retrieved another protein bar, their mainstay. Before this was over, she would never want another, but at least it gave her some energy. She counted how many they had left. Three. A lot of the food never crossed the river with them.

After two hours of standing guard and fending off the mosquitoes, she woke Brody and said, "We better get going."

"How long did you let me sleep?"

"Do you feel better?"

"Yes. How long, Arianna?"

"I gave you enough time to get some rest."

"How about you?"

"Someone had to stand guard, but it's time to go now."

"Time? It's way past the time." He shoved himself up, darkness shrouding him in shadows.

Arianna helped him to rise to his feet. When he put weight on his right leg, he sank down. Quickly she wrapped her arm around him and held him up against her. "What's wrong?" The night made it difficult to see details, only an outline of Brody.

"My ankle. I did something to it."

"Lean on me. Do you think it's broken?"

"No." He shifted and must have put his foot down because he jerked back. "Maybe. But this will not hinder us. We keep moving if I have to hobble the whole way. No matter what, you'll get to Anchorage to testify."

"We'll hobble toward Fairbanks on one condition."

He snorted, but gestured for her to continue.

"You'll let me help you and the first time you can get medical attention you will."

"Yes, ma'am."

"And no lip or you'll hobble all the way to Fairbanks without my help." She thrust the protein bar she'd saved for him into his hand. "You're gonna need all the energy you can get."

"Where's the rifle? I can carry that."

"In several pieces. So it's in the backpack. Can't leave it." Slowly Arianna started down the slope, letting what moonlight there was illuminate their path. "Here's some water to wash the bar down."

He took it. "Did you get any rest?"

"And leave us unguarded? No way. Remember I'm a top-notch bodyguard and don't forget it."

"But I'm supposed to be guarding you."

"So I'm the client?"

"Yeah, so to speak."

"I thought we were a team."

He stopped and twisted toward her, sticking the water bottle in his jean pocket and then settling his hands on her shoulders. "We are and for just a few minutes I could forget about the pain shooting up my leg and the throbbing in my head to enjoy some fun bantering. Thank you, Arianna."

She didn't need to see his face clearly. She felt his gaze on her as though he could pierce through all her barriers and touch her heart, one she had kept protected for four years. She'd been dating the man who'd framed her for giving out intel to the enemy. She'd been used. She wouldn't forget that feeling.

"C'mon. Quit this dillydallying."

He laughed. "Dillydallying?"

"A word my grandmother loved to use with us kids. Quit dillydallying. Move it. She would have made a great drill sergeant." She resumed their hike down the bottom half of the mountain.

"It sounds like you have fond memories of your grandmother. Is she still alive?"

"Yes, as far as I know." Another family member she couldn't see. Sadness enveloped her. A lump rose in her throat, and she swallowed several times, but she couldn't rid herself of the fact she wouldn't be surrounded by her family at the holidays as oftentimes in the past. "She was my role model."

"I'm sorry about what you're going through."

His gentle tone soothed her. In the last few months she'd tried not to think about having to give up all she'd known—people, career—to start new. She'd focused on bringing Rainwater to face justice. But soon she would have to deal with it. For now, though, she would concentrate on getting herself and Brody to Anchorage alive.

In the distance a wolf bayed, reminding her

that all they had now to protect themselves were two Glocks. They wouldn't stop a charging bear.

Midmorning of day two, with the backpack on, Brody leaned over and picked up a piece of wood that would be perfect as a walking stick. "Honest. My ankle is probably only twisted. The ACE bandage gives me some support, and the pain is bearable. I promise," he added when he saw Arianna's skeptical look.

"I see you wince when you put too much weight on that foot."

"That's your imagination."

"Hardly." She scanned the field before them. "I'll feel better when we get across it. I hate being out in the open."

He lifted the binoculars and swept the area before them, noting the dry meadow, the vegetation shorter than usual. He spied some elk at the edge. "Me, too. But it's not far and I don't see anything suspicious."

"That kinda worries me. Nothing since we crossed the mountain. I smell smoke so the fire is probably still burning."

"Forest fires can be hard to contain. When I lived in California, we had one that nearly reached my housing subdivision. I only lived in an apartment, but I certainly didn't want to lose all my possessions. We had to evacuate, and all I could take with me was what I could get in my car."

"What was the first thing you decided to take with you?"

"My laptop with all my pictures on it." He let the binoculars drop to his chest and looked at her, thinking of all she'd had to give up. Much more than he would have if the fire hadn't been contained.

"Of family?"

"Yes. I had everything digitalized."

"You don't have a backup service?"

"Yes. But when I get lonely, I like to look at them." Which had been often of late. He loved Alaska but he felt cut off, especially in the winter months, from his friends and family in the lower states.

"Are your parents alive?"

"My mother's in Florida. She remarried after my dad died. I don't have any siblings, but I have aunts, uncles and cousins. We usually have a big gathering once a year. I try not to miss it." Brody strode next to Arianna, realizing she was keeping her pace slow because of him. He sped up his step. They still had a way to go to get to Fairbanks—not to mention Anchorage.

She matched his faster gait, sliding a glance at him.

"I'm fine. Don't worry about me."

"Who said I was worried?"

"Your expression. It takes more than a fall from a mountain to get me down." He cocked his head and listened, bringing his finger up to his mouth to indicate quiet. The sounds of a helicopter filled the air.

Arianna rotated in a circle, looking up at the sky.

He grabbed her hand and half ran, half limped toward a cluster of trees in the middle of the field that would offer shelter from prying eyes. The whirring noise grew louder. They needed to be under the trees before the helicopter came into view. If someone was looking for them, they would be scanning the terrain.

Three yards away.

Arianna glanced back. "The helicopter's coming from over the mountain."

Brody moved to the side and dropped down, dragging her with him. "This brush should hide us until we get to the trees. We'll have to crawl under it."

With Arianna beside him, he crept on his belly toward the trees, pulling the backpack along the ground in order to fit under the brush.

"This reminds me of my service in the army. I did this many times."

"I can't say I've had the pleasure."

A few feet to the green canopy. He peered

back and realized the chopper would fly right over the pasture.

Even under the trees, he continued to crawl until they were safe in the center of them. Slowly he rose and faced the helicopter as it swooped across the field. He could see its flight path without viewing the chopper because the wind from its rotors stirred up the dust and flattened what vegetation there was. The herd of elk panicked at the noise and ran toward them. They pounded through the stand of spruce, firs and pines.

Pressing up against a large trunk on the backside of a black spruce, he glanced over at Arianna who had done the same thing. His gaze riveted to hers as the helicopter flew overhead and the elk passed by. In the middle of the tense situation a connection sprang up between them. They were in this together. She wasn't a U.S. marshal, and yet he knew she had his back. That feeling heightened his respect for her and the regret about the ordeal she had to go through just for being in the wrong place at the wrong time.

Why, God? This wasn't the first time he'd asked the Lord that question. From all he'd read about Arianna and seen over the past few days, she did a good job helping guard people who needed it. Now she would never be able to go back to that job. How would he feel if he couldn't do what he did?

"Did you see any writing on the helicopter?" Arianna asked, pushing away from the tree she'd hugged. "It was too dense over here."

He had glimpsed only one word through a slit in the green canopy. "In gold lettering I saw the letters CAR. I'm not familiar with a helicopter service with that name, but then I don't know all of them. It wasn't military or government."

"Which means we have to assume it was part of Rainwater's search for us."

"Yep. Let's get into the forest. We'll be safer there."

"I hope you don't regret saying that." She picked up the backpack from the ground. "My turn to carry it." She started out, throwing a grin over her shoulder.

He limped after her, chuckling to himself at her attitude. *Take charge. I can do anything you can. So refreshing.* His usual witnesses weren't anything like Arianna. As he watched her a few feet ahead of him, he liked what he saw. And in that moment he realized he'd better watch where his thoughts were taking him.

Arianna Jackson was off-limits to him. She would testify and then disappear, and he wasn't interested in a relationship without long-term commitment. His relationship with Carla had taught him at least that much.

At the edge of the forest she turned and watched him, her eyes intense, her confidence conveyed in the way she carried herself. Planting one hand on her waist, she grinned. "Marshal Callahan, I do declare you're a slowpoke."

"Is that another phrase your grandma likes to say?"

"Yes, she's a Southern matriarch. She rules her husband and household with a sugarcoated firmness I've never been able to match."

He stepped into the dimness of the forest. "Have you ever been married?"

"Your dossier on me didn't tell you that?"

"All I know is that you're currently single."

"Nope. Although I had two serious boyfriends in my life, neither one led me to the altar."

"What happened?"

Striding next to him because the forest floor didn't have a lot of underbrush, she tilted her head toward him. "I had three older brothers who were standing between any guy and me. They made it tough on any boy in high school or college who was interested. Only one guy was stubborn enough to date me seriously and even he got run off eventually. I had to join the army to get away from their hovering."

"Ah, so your other boyfriend was while you were in the army?"

She nodded.

"Was he in the army, too?"

A frown crunched her forehead. "Yes, though his loyalties lay elsewhere. Thankfully for my sake his dubious character was uncovered before it was too late."

"For the altar?"

"No, for me to be sent to prison."

"Do you want to talk about it?"

"No, it's the past. I want to forget it." The steel thread woven through her words and the pursed lips underscored how hard that was for her.

"But you haven't."

"No, still trying. We haven't talked much about this, but it seems one of your fellow marshals betrayed the location. How does that make you feel?"

"Angry. Determined to find out who did this and make him pay."

"I still feel angry, too, even though I know who was responsible and saw him face justice. I know I should forgive and move on, but I can't. I figure you know what I experienced."

"Yeah, knowing what we're supposed to do and doing it can be two very different things."

"I can't do what God wants me to do. After what happened, I left the army. It wasn't the same for me. My dad thought I should have stuck it out and stayed. Dirk was responsible for sullying my reputation, and although he was caught and stood trial in the end, some still thought I was in it with him. I tried staying but realized all chances of promotion were gone. I disappointed my father and our relationship changed. When we saw each other at family gatherings after that, it was like we were two polite strangers."

"What were you charged with?"

"Selling intel to the enemy." Her frown deepened. "I would never betray my country."

"I'm sorry that happened to you." The sound of a stream nearby echoed through the trees. "I hear water." Brody looked ahead through the binoculars. He pointed to the left. "It's over there. It would be a good way to throw the dogs off if they come this way."

"Stream or river?"

"The wading kind of water. C'mon I'll show you."

As Arianna trudged toward it, she said, "Since I spilled my guts to you—and, by the way, I don't make it a habit to do that—I get to ask you a few questions."

"Okay," he replied warily, noting a gleam in Arianna's gaze.

"I noticed a certain amount of tension between Carla Matthews and you when you came to the cabin. Why?"

"You are good. I thought I covered that pretty well."

"Not well enough. You both tensed up, exchanged looks that could freeze a person."

"I guess I need to work on that."

"I doubt the others noticed. I'm very good at reading the subtle messages. Her eyes narrowed slightly, and she drew herself up straighter. A tic twitched in your jaw, and you made it a point not to look at her."

"Definitely I'm going to have to work on my unreadable expression."

"So why was there tension between you two?"

"I was hoping you would forget the question." He stopped at the edge of a stream, the water flowing gently over round rocks in the bed.

"Nope. Do you really think you can wade through this stream? Look at the rocks."

"I don't have a choice. If they bring the dogs into this forest, they'll pick up our scent. We need to do what we can to confuse the trackers."

"And we probably won't hear them coming." After taking off her tennis shoes and socks, she stepped into the cold water. "Use the stick but also hold on to me."

"What if you go down?"

"Then let go and let me go down. You don't need to twist your other ankle. I'll go first and you follow where I go."

He put his hand on her shoulder and trailed behind her into the water. "We need to walk as much in the center as possible where it's deeper."

"Deeper. Not my favorite word when connected to water."

He squeezed her shoulder. "I'm right here. Nothing is going to happen to you."

"I know. This is nothing compared to a raging river. Have you been coming up with an answer to my earlier question?"

"You're relentless."

"No more than you."

"I'm not going to get any peace until I answer you, am I?"

She laughed. "Don't make it sound like some kind of torture. I've told you things I don't normally share with people I've only known for a few days."

"But what a couple of days they have been. It's not torture so much as me being unaccustomed to sharing at all."

"I bet you were fun on the playground as a kid."

"I'm talking about sharing feelings, not toys. I have a hunch you don't share much either."

"Who am I gonna tell my secrets? My clients? I'm on the road all the time. Not conducive to long-term friendships and I don't share with casual acquaintances."

"How about me?"

She looked back at him, took a step forward then another and nearly went down. Letting go of his stick, he caught her. Her cheeks flamed.

"I'm sorry I distracted you."

Facing him, she narrowed her eyes. "No, you aren't. You're using delaying tactics. Back to the original question."

He sighed. She was right—no point in stalling anymore. Besides, after what she'd shared with him, she deserved his honesty. "Carla and I dated for a while. She was way too intense for me. I realized our relationship, if you could call it that, wasn't leading anywhere and broke it off. She didn't appreciate it. Since we worked together, I couldn't say she was stalking me technically, but there were times when it felt like it. Weird things started happening to me. Calls in the middle of the night. A flat tire when I'd go to work in the morning."

"Flat tires aren't that unusual. I've had my share."

"Three times over five weeks?"

"No. It sounds like someone wasn't happy with you. Is that why you left Los Angeles for Alaska?"

"Not entirely. I lost a witness."

"Like disappeared?"

"No, like was killed."

"Not that this witness is worried, but what happened to the other one?"

He wasn't going to lie to Arianna, but he did not share that dark time with anyone. "Nothing to concern you. The situations are totally different."

As they rounded a bend in the stream, Arianna halted, then moved back. "I see the top of a car on the left side up ahead."

He stepped around her, brought the binoculars up and surveyed the situation. "There's a tent. I don't see anyone though. It may be campers."

"Or?"

"Or someone looking for us."

SIX

"Make a wide berth around them?" Arianna asked, searching the terrain for any sign of the people connected to the car.

"Let's check them out more closely. They could be our way out of here. The best way to evade dogs is a car. Can't track us when the scent vanishes."

Arianna eyed the steep incline on the left side of the creek. "How's your foot?"

"Numb from the cold water, but I think that's helped it. Like a pack of ice."

She nodded toward their route out of the stream. "I'll go first, and if you need help up the slope, I can give you a hand."

Picking her way through the rocky bottom, she made it to the side, Brody right behind her. "This should be easy after the mountain."

She grabbed hold of the trunk of a small tree and used it to hoist herself up and over to the forest floor above the creek. Favoring his good leg, Brody followed suit, rolled over and sat up to put his socks and boots on over his soaking wet ACE bandage. Arianna was on her feet and peering around the bend in the stream toward the car and campsite.

"What do you think?" Brody asked, close to her ear.

She swallowed her gasp at his sudden quiet appearance next to her. "Still don't see anyone. Maybe they're hunting or fishing. We'll need to go closer."

Using the foliage and tree trunks to hide them, Brody and she sneaked closer. She focused her attention on the campsite while he scoured the area for any sign of the car's owner.

Fifteen yards away from their objective a rustling sound to the right near the camp stilled Arianna's movements. A man and woman around the age of fifty came into the small clearing where the tent was pitched. He carried a rifle and they both had binoculars around their necks.

Arianna ducked back deeper into the underbrush. "What do you think? After us or two campers on holiday?"

He fixed his gaze on the couple. "I see a camera in the woman's hand. At first glance they seem all right."

"But…"

"Appearances can be deceiving. You and I have both encountered that in our lives."

Immediately Arianna thought of Dirk and then the latest person—the marshal who had betrayed her location. "Let's move closer and listen to what they're talking about. I'm not quite ready to just walk into their camp without more info."

"I like how you think—cautiously."

"There's time for action and time for waiting and seeing what happens."

"Not for long. We can't stay anyplace long."

"Why not?" asked a low-pitched female voice behind them.

Arianna peered over her shoulder. A young woman, no more than twenty, stood with her shotgun aimed at them. Arianna thought of going for her weapon at her side.

"I wouldn't if I were you," the girl said. "Both of you turn around slowly and start doing some explaining."

When Brody was fully around and facing the stranger, he nodded toward the gun. "Why don't you point that thing somewhere else?"

"I will when you explain what you meant by not staying long in a place."

"There's a forest fire not far from here. We've been running from it since yesterday. We had to leave our camping equipment and about everything we had and make a run for it. The last we saw the fire, the wind was blowing it this way. I'm surprised to find anyone here," Brody said, using his soft, nonthreatening voice.

The young woman relaxed slightly. "I smelled smoke. That's why I went up the tree to see if I could find out where it was coming from."

"Oh, then you saw the fire." Arianna watched the girl's body language intently. The more she looked at her the more she thought she was probably a teenager.

"Yep, but the wind has changed directions. It's blowing more directly north now. I think we'll be safe." The girl gestured with her shotgun. "If you're out here, those side arms ain't nearly as effective as a rifle or shotgun, especially for bears. We camp here every year and a couple of times bears have been a problem."

"Jane, who are you talking to?" a male voice asked.

"That's my grandpa," Jane said to them, then shouted, "A couple running from the fire I seen." Again she made a motion with her gun. "C'mon. I'll introduce you to my grandparents. They don't live too far from here."

Arianna looked at Brody, who nodded. "We'd love to meet them."

With her arms out to indicate she wasn't

reaching for her Glock, Arianna slowly rose. Brody did the same.

"Go ahead," Jane said, pointing toward the campsite, her shotgun still aimed at them.

When Arianna passed close to Brody, she whispered, "I'm not liking the gun pointed at us."

"Me, either." He slid a look back as he limped toward the campsite.

"What's wrong, mister?" Jane asked while trailing behind them.

"I fell and twisted my ankle."

"Running from the fire?"

"Yes."

As they entered the campsite, the man stood near the fire pit with his rifle up and fixed on Brody. It had been strained before with the teenager, but now the tension shot up like the fire devouring the forest across the river.

As Brody bridged the distance to the older man, he said, "That's as far as you come. Who are you?"

"I'm B.J. and this is my wife, Anna. I understand from your granddaughter you live around here."

He scowled. "What of it?"

Jane had been downright friendly compared to her grandfather. Arianna glanced at the woman not far from the man. Her hard expression, gaze glued to Arianna, did nothing to alleviate the stress.

"Nothing. Just trying to carry on a conversation. That coffee on the fire smells wonderful."

"Jane, git the rope. I think these two are who those officers were looking for."

"We're not running from the law but the fire." Arianna clenched her hands at her side, more worried about the two officers than this couple and their granddaughter.

Brody sidled closer to Arianna. "What makes you think that, sir?"

"You fit the description of the fugitives. You're wanted for starting that fire. If the wind had shifted, my home would be in the middle of it."

"What law enforcement officers?"

"State troopers. They came through this morning early."

Jane appeared at her grandfather's side, holding a length of rope.

Arianna exchanged a look with Brody. Were those Rainwater's men dressed as state troopers or did someone truly think she and Brody were behind the fire? But that didn't make sense. Wouldn't the U.S. Marshals Service step in and inform them about what was going on?

"Both of you take out your guns slow and easy then toss them over here," Grandpa said, lifting his rifle higher and aiming at Brody while Jane pointed hers at Arianna. "No shenanigans. First B.J. then Anna." He slurred their fake names as though he didn't believe a word they had said.

All the while Brody followed the older man's directions, Arianna assessed the situation, trying to find a way to get the upper hand. None presented itself without one or both of them being shot before she could use her Glock.

"Jane and Maude, tie them up. Remember I have the rifle trained on you two. I kilt a charging bear by hitting it between the eyes. Girls, use that tree over there."

"What are you gonna do with us?" Arianna knew no good would come from being turned over to those "state troopers."

"Send Maude and my granddaughter to tell those state troopers about you."

"Where are they?" Brody asked as Grandma Maude jerked him toward the tree.

"Out on the highway not too far from here. They told us they have some kind of command post. If I seen anything I was to let them know."

"They just came up to you and asked you to help them?" Arianna uncurled her hands, trying to relax herself in order to move at a second's notice. The first opportunity…

"No, I saw them in their uniforms. I asked

them. They were mighty surprised to see me and Maude bird watching."

"Are you sure they were real state troopers?" Arianna asked as Jane gestured for her to move to where Brody was now tied against the trunk.

"They were. I seen state troopers before, and they looked just like them. Maude, make sure he's tied tight. Don't want them getting away. Jane, the same with her."

Jane yanked the rope until it cut into Arianna's wrists. When Maude walked back toward her husband, Arianna whispered, "Jane, we aren't criminals. We were running from the fire and trying to get to the highway. Please help us."

"I can't. I was up in the tree. I saw those two men. Grandpa doesn't lie."

"What's taking ya so long, girl? You and your grandma need to go git help."

Jane peered around the tree trunk. "Just making sure she ain't going nowhere."

"Jane, if you bring those men back here, they'll kill us and maybe you all, too."

Jane's eyes widened. "Why? We ain't done nothing wrong."

"Neither have we."

Jane bolted to her feet. "They ain't going nowhere, Grandpa."

"Good. Check their pockets. Make sure they don't have anything they can use to get free."

Jane patted her down and found the money and the switchblade Arianna had, then turned her attention to Brody. She removed his wallet but didn't look at it. Jane hurried to her grandparents. "They don't have nothing now."

"Good. I think I'm going with you two. We'll tell them where these two are and then go home. It's getting late anyway and we'll let the state troopers take care of these criminals. Let's pack up."

Arianna craned her neck around to see the family packing up and tearing down their tent probably in record time. "What are we gonna do? She took my knife."

"I'm working on it."

"The ropes?"

"Yep."

"I can't budge mine. Jane followed her grandpa's instructions to a tee. In fact, my hands are starting to feel numb."

"Grandma doesn't have as much strength as Jane. I might be able to work these loose."

The sound of the car starting filled the clearing. Out of the corner of her eye she glimpsed the green vehicle drive away. "At least we know which way the highway is."

"That's the highway where the *state troopers* have set up a command post."

"Then it's probably not the way to get to Fairbanks."

"It's the only way out of here going that way. On the bright side, they left us our backpack."

"The guns, too?"

Brody chuckled. "If only that were the case. No, they took them."

"So even if we can get away, we have no weapons or money." Arianna twisted her hands over and over to try and make the rope give some. It was cooperating—barely. "How are you coming with getting free?"

"It may be a while. Grandma was stronger than I thought."

"How long do you figure we have?"

"It's hard to tell. I doubt this is far from the highway, but I don't know where this command post is."

"Could it be the real state troopers?"

"Notice Grandpa didn't mention if the troopers gave our names, just our description, so I guess it could be. The U.S. Marshals Service would be careful about what they reveal. The site was compromised. That will make them cautious about who to trust, especially in this high profile of a case. Rainwater has a lot of influence. We probably don't know how deep and wide it goes."

"That's not reassuring."

"It wasn't meant to be."

Arianna worked hard to loosen the ropes around her hands. If she got them off, then she could get out from under the one around their chests and untie the twine around her feet. As she moved, the rough bark dug into her back. A small price to pay if they could release themselves.

A noise penetrated her desperation to undo the ropes. A car. "That was fast. The command post must have been close. Or maybe it's someone else, and we can convince them we've been robbed, which is the truth. I had four hundred dollars." She yanked herself around as far as she could to see the vehicle when it appeared. The rope cut into her chest, making breathing difficult.

"What were you going to do with four hundred dollars? This trip to Alaska was all paid for by the U.S. Marshals Service. You certainly weren't going shopping or sightseeing."

"I've been on better paid vacations than this one. It was a comfort for me just in case something like this happened. If I needed to run, at least I had some money to help me disappear."

"I suggest we start praying this is the real state troopers and no one on Rainwater's payroll."

As the sound grew closer, Arianna did pray. At the moment she couldn't get herself out of the mess she was in without the Lord's intervention. Tied to the tree as they were, they were a great target for any of Rainwater's men who wanted to practice their shooting.

Friend or foe? Please, Lord, let it be a friend coming.

The front of the vehicle came into view— green-colored. Grandpa, Maude and Jane had returned. Were they alone? Her heartbeat slowed to a throb as she waited to see who was in the car other than their three captors. Although they had tied them up, the family was a better option than fake highway patrol officers.

But even when the vehicle came fully around the bend, the dark windows made it impossible to see inside. Arianna slumped back against the rough bark, dragging smoke-scented air into her lungs.

"If it's just them returning, we need to get them to untie us," Brody said from the other side of the tree.

"Jane might listen. As I talked to her, she paused when she was tying me up. I don't think she liked the idea of doing it."

"But she follows her grandpa's orders."

She heard the car come to a stop. How in the world did she ever think that she could do this alone? While in some tough situations in the army, she hadn't thought she could get by without God's protection. Even while she was awaiting trial in a prison cell, she'd turned to Him. She'd allowed her bitterness toward Dirk rule her life. To make her doubt the Lord.

A door opened—the noise carrying in the quiet clearing. Arianna tensed. "What's going on?"

"It's only the family returning," Brody murmured, surprise in his voice.

"That's a good sign. Maybe they couldn't find the command post because there wasn't one."

"They weren't gone long enough to have gone far. Grandpa is heading this way."

"With his rifle?" Arianna whispered.

"Yes, but pointed down. I don't think he goes anywhere without it."

The crunch of the other man's footsteps resonated through the forest. Coming nearer. Was this good or bad? The thump of her heartbeat hammered against her skull. The past few days' tension gripped her.

"Why didn't you tell me you were a U.S. Marshal?" Grandpa asked, tightness in the question.

"You finally looked at my wallet?"

"Yep. When Jane showed me, I turned around." The older man came around so Arianna could see him, too. "Are you one, too? Where is your ID? Jane didn't find any on you."

"Most of my belongings burned in the fire, but I'm not a marshal."

"Who are you?"

"I told you. She's Anna. We were camping like you when the fire hit. We aren't the people the state troopers are looking for. In fact, there has been a bulletin I've seen about someone pretending to be a state trooper then robbing people. Did the ones you talked to show you an ID and badge?"

Grandpa scratched his balding head. "Well, now that I think about it, no they didn't. I just assumed since they were dressed in uniform. You think they weren't state troopers?"

"Maybe. What kind of description did they give for the couple they were looking for?"

"A man and woman about thirty or so. The woman is a blonde while the man had dark brown hair."

"That could fit a lot of people. But it isn't us."

"I don't know. You should have said something to me."

Arianna saw the doubt flitter across Grandpa's face. He took a step back, raising his gun. "We might as well tell him the whole truth. I'm a U.S. marshal, too. That was why I was armed. All I can say is that my partner and I are on a case we can't talk about." She hated to lie, but she had no choice when their lives were on the line.

"Why didn't you tell me before I left you tied up?"

"If you found there was a command post and the state troopers were real, we figured we would explain to them when they came," Brody said in an even, patient voice.

"If I hadn't found them, what if I had just kept driving and went home?"

"We knew you weren't that kind of man. We could see you were only trying to do the right thing." Arianna bent toward Grandpa, the rope about her chest only allowing her to go a few inches. "We need to keep our presence hush-hush. Can you do that?" She spoke in low tones as if she were imparting top secret intel to the man.

Sweat popping out on his forehead, Grandpa put the rifle on the ground, knelt next to Arianna and began untying her. "I won't say a word, not even to Maude and Jane." He glanced at his family leaning against the car, Jane's arms crossed over her chest, chewing on her bottom lip. "You're B.J. and Anna on vacation. That's all they need to know."

"I appreciate that."

As Grandpa turned to free Brody, Arianna loosened the rope about her feet, then rubbed her chafed skin, especially around her wrists, and rose. For a few seconds she debated whether to go for the rifle or not. It was close by the man's feet, but that move might produce results that would make this situation worse. She would stick with her story and hope they got out of this alive and not turned in to the "authorities." The two state troopers who'd stopped by earlier in the day were still out there. Looking for them.

Brody stood and offered his hand to Grandpa. "Thanks for coming back. We need citizens who try to do the right thing."

Grandpa beamed, straightening his shoulders even more. After he picked up his rifle, he started for his car. "We'll give you a ride wherever you need to go," he said then paused, rotated toward them and continued in a low voice, "Unless you need to stay because of your job."

Brody sent Arianna a conspiratorial look followed by a wink, which Grandpa didn't see. "The fire has changed everything. We need to get back to the headquarters where the operation is running. A ride to Fairbanks would be great. From there we can get where we need to go, but if anyone asks, I hope you can keep it quiet."

"I understand. Not a word from me, especially since you're being so nice after I had you tied up. One of my favorite shows to watch is about the U.S. Marshals Service. I certainly know what you two do to keep this country safe. Keep up the good work." He turned to his family and announced, "We're taking them part of the way to their destination."

Jane glanced up through her long bangs. "You ain't mad at me—us?"

"No, you all thought you had two criminals, and you did something about that." Arianna forced a big smile to her lips, not letting down her guard one bit, especially since they still had to drive by the "command post."

But twenty minutes later, Grandpa threw a look over his shoulder at Brody and said, "The command post should have been back there. You were right. Those two were phony state troopers. I should call—"

"That's okay. I'll inform the right authorities when we get to our destination. Just remember in the future to always ask for a badge and ID and look at it closely."

"I'll remember that." Grandpa touched his temple. "It don't take but once for me to learn a lesson. Remember what B.J. said, Jane."

"Yes, Grandpa." Jane dug into her pocket and withdrew the switchblade, running her fingers up and down the knife casing. "This is yours. I forgot to give it back with the money."

Arianna curled her hand around Jane's outreached one. "You keep it. I imagine you can find a use for it living in the woods."

Jane's expression brightened, a grin spreading across her face. "When I go hunting, it'll help me skin the critters. We use almost every part of the animals I bring home."

"Yep, keeps us fed well," Maude finally spoke after being quiet since they got into the car.

"Our favorite is rabbit stew," Grandpa added.

Hunting had never appealed to Arianna, even more so with her job. She'd seen what her clients had gone through being hunted by someone who intended to kill them. Having traveled all over the world, she knew many people still hunted for their food. But she'd never been able to go hunting with her dad or brothers in the mountains of North Carolina.

Brody slid his hand over hers on the seat between them in the back of the car. She spied the raw skin on his wrist from the rope. Its sight only reinforced the ordeal they had been through so far. Exhaustion embedded itself in the marrow of her bones.

Brody leaned toward her ear and said, "Rest. It's your turn. I'll stay alert."

Arianna laid her head back against the cushion. With Brody next to her, watching over her, she would be fine. That and the fact she felt the Lord was watching over her, too. Sleep whisked her away almost instantly.

Arianna snuggled up against Brody as they entered the outskirts of Fairbanks. She'd fallen asleep right away, and other than rolling her head and resting it against his shoulder, she'd hardly moved. Even when he'd slung his arm around her and pressed her against him, allowing his body to pillow her in her sleep, she'd stayed deep in a dream world.

"Where to, B.J.?" Fred—Grandpa had given Brody his name partway through the trip— asked from the driver's seat.

"Could you take us to the train station on Johansen Expressway?"

"Yep. I know where it is. My cousin came in on the train a few months back to visit us."

Arianna stirred within the crook of his arm. Her eyes blinked open. A few seconds passed before she reacted to being cradled along his side. She didn't move away, but instead smiled at him. "I was tired. How long was I asleep?"

"An hour and a half," Fred answered from the front. "B.J. told us how long you two had been evading the fire. Heard on the radio they're sending in firefighters from all over to help contain it. Thank the Lord, the winds are still blowing it away from our cabin."

Arianna sat up straight. "That's good. Hopefully the wind will die down, and they'll be able to put the fire out. That area is beautiful."

"Yep, it sure is. Maude and me have lived there for twenty years. It's about all that Jane knows. She came to live with us when she was a baby."

As Fred expounded on what he'd taught his granddaughter, Brody kept his gaze fixed on the area they were passing through. He didn't know Fairbanks that well, but he knew its basic layout.

Ten minutes later when Fred pulled up near the Fairbanks train depot, the clock on the tower indicated it was almost three. Brody glimpsed a black SUV parked near the depot with two men in it. He had a bad feeling about them. "Stop here. We'll walk the rest of the way."

"Sure, but we can pull right up to the door if you want. Or we can take you to the airport or bus station."

"No, this is fine." Brody opened the door, grabbed the backpack at his feet and climbed out of the car. He leaned back in to help Arianna out.

"Sure, I understand." Fred winked. "We three will forget we even saw you two. Mum's the word."

"Thank you. We appreciate your help." Arianna slid across the seat and stood next to Brody. "I'll be praying your cabin remains untouched."

"You do that, Anna," Fred said as she shut the door.

Brody waited until the green car disappeared from view before grasping Arianna's hand and starting in the opposite direction from the train station.

"This isn't exactly in the middle of downtown."

"No, but the town isn't far. We'll find a restaurant to eat at where we won't look too much out of place. Our appearances leave something to be desired."

"I should be offended," Arianna said with a laugh, "but I can still smell the smoke on these clothes. I hope we can find some place to change and take a shower. Do you think we can take a chance on a hotel room?"

"No, but I have an idea. Someone we can trust to help. Charlie Owens. He's a retired FBI agent. I'm sure he still has contacts. He's been in Alaska a long time and only recently retired."

"Why him?" Arianna asked as they crossed a street, getting closer to the downtown area.

"I saved his life last year. We were working the same case. We've kept in touch since he left the FBI, but it's not common knowledge—nor is the fact that I pushed him out of the way of a bullet. No one needed to know Charlie was caught unaware. He was leaving the FBI in a few weeks, and I wanted nothing to take away from that, so I left it out of the report. He used to live in Anchorage but moved up here."

"I'm not sure about that. It might be safer to find some hotel and pay cash for a room."

"I'm pretty sure the train station was being watched as all the other ways out of Fairbanks. I wouldn't be surprised if the surrounding towns have people in them looking for us. You're very important to Rainwater. We don't know which hotel clerks have been paid off to alert someone if two people fitting our description come in to rent a room."

"Then we'll find some place in a park to sleep."

"I'm sure all areas are being checked. That's what I would do if I was looking for a fugitive."

"Okay, you've convinced me. If you trust Charlie Owens, then fine. Just don't plan on me trusting him. With all you've said, should we even risk going somewhere to eat?"

"Good point. I think that was my hunger speaking back there." Brody looked up and down the street, saw a store that might have a pay phone and continued. "Let me call him. See if he's home. If not, maybe we could disguise ourselves and still go to a restaurant and eat. I think it would be better than wandering around Fairbanks until I can get hold of Charlie."

"I can put my hair up, wear sunglasses and put a hoodie on. That ought to change my appearance enough."

"C'mon. Let's go in here. You shop for the sunglasses while I call Charlie." He walked down the aisle toward the pay phone in back. "Stay in my sight."

Brody made the call after getting his friend's number from information. He let it ring until it went to Charlie's answering machine. Deciding not to leave a message, he hung up.

Arianna popped up next to him with a pair of big sunglasses on. "How do I look?"

"That's good. Your eyes are very distinctive—and beautiful."

Two rosy patches graced her cheeks.

"You definitely have to do something about your hair. That's a dead giveaway even from a distance."

"I'm not cutting it. I'll wear a wig before I do that. I kept it short in the army. This is four years of my hair growing out."

"And I like it. Let's see if there's a hat or wig in this store."

"I saw a display of throwaway phones. We

could purchase one of them. They aren't easily traceable, and then we don't have to find a pay phone. They aren't as common as they used to be."

"Good point. Let's grab what we need and clean up the best we can in the store's restrooms. I'll keep calling Charlie every half an hour until we get him."

Thirty minutes later, Brody walked out of the store with his arm around her as if they were in a relationship. The people looking for them might not think of them as a couple. They kept to the back streets, assessing the area where they were going before making a move. When Brody found North Diner, it was nearly deserted because it was in between lunch and dinner. He took a booth at the back with a good view of the entrance that was close to the restroom and a back way out of the restaurant.

Arianna opened her menu. "I'm starved. I could eat one of everything on this menu. I don't think I want to see a protein bar anytime soon."

After they placed their orders with the young waitress, Brody pulled out the throwaway cell phone and made another call to Charlie. His friend answered on the third ring, much to Brody's relief. He'd begun to think Charlie was out of town.

Brody checked the restaurant for anyone

nearby who could overhear the conversation and then said low into the cell, "I need your help."

"I told you anytime you did to call. Does this have anything to do with what is happening northwest of Fairbanks? I've heard some chatter about recovering five bodies—murder victims. The fire destroyed most of the evidence. The authorities are looking for any other people who were caught in the forest fire."

"Do they know how the blaze started?"

"A dropped cigarette and a dry forest. But that's speculation. There was one body burned worse than the others. So are you involved?"

"I need to lie low. I don't want anyone to know I'm here. Not even the U.S. Marshals Service. Can you help?"

Charlie emitted a soft whistle. "This sounds serious."

"Lives are at stake."

"Where are you? I'll come pick you up."

Brody gave him the address of North Diner. "There's an alley out back of the restaurant. I'll be waiting there. How long will you be?"

"Twenty minutes."

"What kind of car do you drive?"

"A white Jeep. It's seen better days."

"Thanks, Charlie. See you in twenty." When Brody hung up, he continued. "I'm going to let the waitress know we want everything to go."

Brody strode to the counter and found his waitress. "We need to leave. We'll take the food to go and I'll pay for it now."

After the transaction was completed, Brody walked by the picture window, searching the street out front. A black SUV with dark windows drove slowly by. He ducked back, the hairs on his nape tingling. At the side of the window, he peered out to see where the SUV was going. It stopped and a woman climbed out of the passenger seat. He stared at Carla Matthews across the road as she went into a small hotel.

Was Carla here as a U.S. Marshal or one of Rainwater's lackeys?

SEVEN

Brody hurried to the counter. "Is the food ready?"

"In just a minute," the waitress said and went back into the kitchen.

Arianna rose with the backpack in hand. Looking at her disguise, he couldn't tell clearly she was Arianna Jackson, the witness the U.S. Marshals Service and Rainwater's men were searching for. He waved for her to head back toward the restrooms, making a motion to turn away from them. As she did, the waitress brought out a sack with the food in it. He left and limped after Arianna toward the back while the waitress returned to the kitchen.

Outside in the alley, Brody paced. "Charlie should be here soon. Stand by the door so anyone driving by won't see you."

"How about you?"

He stepped into the entrance of a shop on the other side of the alley. "There was a black SUV that dropped Carla off at the end of the block. They're canvassing the street. If they are, then Rainwater's men are here, too."

"Do you think Carla is the mole?"

"Maybe. And since I don't know, we can't approach her."

"Do you think someone let them know we're in Fairbanks?"

"Maybe. Fred Franklin might have decided to call the U.S. Marshals Service after all. If he did, then whoever gave up your location probably knows by now that the Franklins dropped us at the Fairbanks train station." Brody peeked around the brick wall down the alley on both side. He spied a black SUV pass on the street on his left side and darted back against the store's door.

"What's wrong?"

"Another SUV. Maybe another marshal is being dropped off on the next street. Either way, this is not good."

"Fairbanks is the closest major town from where we were. That may be why they're searching even though it's away from Anchorage. Fairbanks has better transportation to get us to Anchorage. They'll know we can't walk there and get there in time for the trial."

Brody plowed his fingers through his hair. "Yeah, I know, but I hate not knowing who to trust." In the past he'd trusted the members of his team. How would he be able to after this?

The sound of a car turning into the alley announced they weren't alone. Under his light jacket, Brody put his hand on his gun and inched forward to take a peek at what kind of vehicle was coming toward them. His rigid body relaxed when he saw a white Jeep.

"It's Charlie, but don't come out until I tell you to. If there's a problem, duck back into the diner. Hide in the restroom." Brody stepped out of the doorway to the store and stood several yards down the alley for Charlie to stop. He didn't want his friend to see Arianna until he'd talked with Charlie.

Brody slipped into the front passenger's seat and angled his body toward the former FBI agent. "Retirement has been kind to you."

"Do we have time for this chitchat? What's up? Why are you running from your own people? I saw a marshal I know get out of an SUV two blocks over."

"Who?"

"Ted Banks. He's hard to miss."

"I'll tell you everything when we get out of here and to your house."

Charlie put his hand on the stick shift to put the vehicle into drive.

"Wait. There's another passenger."

"The witness in Rainwater's trial?"

Brody nodded, got out of the car and said, "It's okay. Hurry."

Arianna darted out of the diner's doorway and jogged toward the Jeep, looking behind her then in front of her. She slid into the backseat as Brody took the one next to her.

"Charlie, this is Arianna, the witness I need to get to Anchorage ASAP to testify at Rainwater's trial."

"Nice to meet you," Charlie said to Arianna, watching her through the rearview mirror. "We'll talk when I get you to a friend's house— I'm watching it for him while he's salmon fishing. I suggest both of you get down until we arrive there."

Arianna scrunched down on the floor, facing Brody. He took her hand and held it. "Charlie saw Ted Banks a few blocks over so it's not just Carla here. Five bodies were found around the cabin—one burned worse than the others. He thinks that one was near the point of origin."

"Just passed another car that looks suspicious," Charlie said from the font seat. He made a turn then continued. "The firefighters have ruled out a lightning strike and they can't find any evidence of an accelerant being used, especially where they think the fire started. The guy I talked with speculated it was a cigarette."

Arianna frowned. "An accident?"

"We thought it might have been set deliberately, but are you saying that might not be the case?" Brody asked Charlie.

"With a cigarette it could still be deliberate. That way the fire would take a while to catch. It would give the person who set it time to get out of the area."

Arianna caught Brody's gaze. "It makes more sense if it was an accident. Burning the cabin doesn't accomplish anything other than calling attention to the place."

"Possibly. Or maybe there was something they wanted to cover up."

"Five bodies were found. That must mean they found Kevin."

"Unless there was someone we didn't know about."

"Were all the bodies found at the cabin?" Arianna asked Charlie as he pulled up to a stoplight.

The former FBI agent shifted as though he were staring out the side window. "The firefighter didn't say. I could find out."

"Only if it doesn't seem suspicious. I wouldn't want anyone paying you a visit." Brody moved to ease the pressure on his sore ankle.

"Believe me, I don't either. We're almost at

my friend's house. Well, more like a cabin. I hope you don't mind staying in a rustic place."

Arianna laughed. "You should have seen where we've been. Anywhere with a roof over our heads and running water that isn't a stream is a big step up."

"There's a roof, running water, and even an indoor bathroom."

"Oh, that sounds luxurious. Is there a bed with a soft mattress?"

"Yeah, plus a couch."

The smile that graced Arianna's face lit her features with radiance. Her look appealed to Brody—way too much if he stopped to think about it. She was strictly a professional concern. Once she left Alaska after testifying, he could get back to his life—that was, if they made it to Anchorage alive.

She reached out to him and grazed her fingertips down his jaw. "We're gonna make it. We've got your friend's help. Rainwater isn't going to win."

The light touch of her hand on his face doubled his pulse rate. His throat thickened with emotions he never allowed on a job. He cared. She was cheering him up. Usually he was trying to do that with his witnesses, especially when the reality of their situation really sank in. All the waiting for the trial gave the witnesses time to think. To realize their lives would be radically different because they were doing the right thing.

"We're here. He doesn't have any neighbors close by, but I'm still going to park around back in his garage. That's what he calls it, at least. I call it a lean-to about to collapse."

Brody rose in the seat. "And you're parking your Jeep in there?"

"Out of sight is better than announcing to everyone where I am—just in case they run down people you know in the area to see if you've gotten in touch with them."

"Won't anyone think it's strange you're gone from your home?" Arianna climbed from the Jeep after Charlie parked it in a shed that really did look like it would blow down in a strong wind.

"Not my friends. They know I often just pick up and go somewhere. That's what retirement is all about."

"Then I hope they ask your friends."

"Either way, we can't stay for long. Tomorrow we'll have to figure out a way to Anchorage," Brody said as he limped toward Charlie's friend's place.

"I might have a way to get you there. I have a friend who has a ranch. She raises cattle and horses. She's been wanting me to help her take some horses down south. I'd told her I could do it at the end of the week. I'll call her and see about tomorrow." Charlie unlocked the door of the cabin. "This is the only way in and out, except the windows."

Stepping inside, Brody assessed the space, noting where the windows were and how easy they would be to access. "We have dinner in these bags. I think Arianna ordered half the menu, so there'll be plenty for all of us. I hope you're hungry."

Charlie's laughter filled the large living room that flowed into the kitchen. "Are you kidding? You've seen me eat out. I've been known to finish a twenty-five ounce steak and want more."

Arianna dropped the backpack by the brown couch then took the two sacks from Brody. "I'll go get this reheated. Dinner won't be long."

"Good. I'll call Willow and see about the horses for tomorrow." Charlie started to pick up the phone on an end table.

"Wait. Use my cell. It's not traceable."

Charlie hiked an eyebrow. "You really are worried someone will find you."

"This is important. Three of Rainwater's men found us at the safe cabin. If she doesn't testify, he'll be acquitted. She's most of the state's case against him."

"Yeah, I've been reading about the case. A

nasty man. He may live in Anchorage, but he has his hand in a lot of things all over the state."

While Arianna strode to the kitchen and took the food out of the sacks, Charlie made the call to Willow. Most of the conversation took place on the other end. A faint flush brushed Charlie's cheeks. He turned away from Brody to finish what he was saying to the woman. Interesting. Charlie had never been married before, but from what he'd seen, his friend was attracted to Willow.

Charlie hung up and handed the cell back to Brody. "We're good for tomorrow. I'll go to the ranch and pick up the horses at seven, then come back here to get you two. At first Willow wanted to come with me. I discouraged her and reminded her about the fire west of here. She needs to be on her ranch if there's a problem and they can't contain it."

"She lives that close?"

"No, but I had to think of something to keep her home. Willow is the most delicate woman I know. Fragile actually. She's been sick until recently. Cancer. She's finally getting her life back."

"You care about her?"

Charlie's mouth twisted into a look that wasn't a frown but not a smile either. "Yeah, I guess I do. She's planning a special dinner when

I get back. I told her I might be in Anchorage for a few days after I deliver the horses. I figure you're going to need all the help you can get."

"It won't be easy getting to Anchorage. I don't know who to trust, even in my own office."

Charlie stared at Arianna. "We'll get her to the courthouse."

Brody hoped so. He wasn't going to lose a witness, especially not Arianna. In spite of his best intentions, there was something about her that he liked—a lot.

Refreshed after a meal and a shower, Arianna stood in front of the mirror in the bathroom, examining the cuts on her face. She looked like she'd gone through a battle. In one way she had. She was fighting for her life—and Brody's.

But there was hope. Charlie had a way to Anchorage that might not alert the wrong people. She had no choice. If she didn't testify against Rainwater, she would never have a chance of surviving. She closed her eyes and tried to imagine a life in the Witness Protection Program. A new name. A new job. A new home. Since she left her childhood house, she never really had a place she could call home. Now she would. But what did she want to do with that life?

When she opened her eyes and stared again

at herself in the mirror, no answers came to mind. That scared her more than anything. The unknown.

Then she remembered something her grandmother had told her when she was a child. When she was scared, fix her thoughts on the Lord. He was always there for her, rooting for her, supporting her so she really never was alone.

She'd forgotten that these past four years while trying to control her life, needing no one. Now she needed others to keep her alive, but mostly she needed the Lord to give her the hope it would be all right.

A knock at the door pulled her from her thoughts. "Yes?"

"Are you okay?" Brody's voice held the concern she'd come to cherish.

"Yes."

"Charlie has some information on what's going down at the cabin."

"Coming." Arianna ran a brush through her hair, putting it up into a ponytail.

When she entered the living room, Brody and Charlie stopped talking and looked at her. Brody's warm perusal caused flutters in her stomach. She sat near him on the couch while Charlie settled across from them in a chair.

"What have you discovered?" Arianna couldn't stop thinking about how Brody had been there for her every step of the way. Yes, it was his job, but she might not be alive today if he didn't do his job so well.

"A sixth man was found dead near the cabin. I have a friend who worked the fire. He said the sixth person was not far from the body at the edge of the tree line."

"The other four bodies were in or right outside the cabin?"

"Yes, the only way they'll be able to ID any of the bodies is with dental records, according to my friend."

"So they aren't sure who is dead, except they know they're all male," Brody said, tapping his hand against the arm of the couch. He looked at Arianna. "The U.S. Marshals Service doesn't know if you're dead somewhere else or if you fled by yourself. Right now they think I could be any one of the six men."

"But Rainwater's men know I wasn't killed, that I fled."

Brody kneaded his nape. "Probably, but we aren't sure what they know. If they saw the cabin before it burned, yes they know. By the two fake state troopers who talked with the Franklins, we have to assume they know that you and a marshal are gone. That might give us an edge. They aren't sure who you're with."

"We know people are looking for us. That much is a definite."

"Yes, there's a widespread manhunt out for Arianna Jackson, possibly with a male accompanying her." Charlie pushed to his feet and walked into the kitchen. "Anyone want some coffee?"

"No, I won't get any sleep tonight." Arianna shifted toward Brody. "I'll take the first watch. You need to get some rest."

"You mean my two hours late last night wasn't enough?" he said in dead seriousness.

She smiled. "I know you're a marshal with superpowers, but going without sleep isn't one of them. Tomorrow will be a big day for us. We'll either make it to Anchorage or…" She couldn't quite say the alternative. Their lives were on the line but so was Charlie's now.

"I know, and my body is totally agreeing with you. Sleep is a priority."

"Yeah, that's why I'm going to stand guard tonight. I got eight hours last night," Charlie said as he folded his large bulk into the chair and took a sip of his coffee.

"Tell you what, friend. Arianna will take the first two hours and I'll take the last two. You can stand guard for the four hours between."

"Done. Now let's talk about why you're keeping this from your own people. Who do you think is the mole?"

Brody's forehead creased, his jaw tensed. "It could be any one of the marshals on the first team or my team. It could be someone higher up."

"Are you sure it was a marshal?"

"Not one hundred percent, but how else can I explain the breach in our location? Our attackers had a map—they knew exactly where we were. It could have been Kevin because he would have had to radio in for Mark to open the door. Mark wouldn't have opened it without that. But then it could have been Mark, and after they took out Kevin, he let them into the cabin."

Arianna saw the anger and sadness warring for dominance on Brody's expression. "So you think it's most likely the inside man was one of the two marshals on your team?" she asked.

"It could still be someone from the first team. The word phrase we use if we're being forced to call in is the same for the operation. Those three marshals knew that phrase so one of them could have told Rainwater's men."

"What was the phrase?" Arianna knew the emotions Brody was struggling with. She'd dealt with the same ones with Dirk—was still dealing with them.

"All clear. No bear sightings." Brody's scowl

deepened. "Kevin and Mark are dead. If one of them was the mole, Rainwater was definitely leaving no one around to testify against him."

"Not a bad strategy for the man who is in jail because Thomas Perkins was selling him out." All because of money and greed. Arianna squeezed her hands into tight fists, her fingernails digging into her palms.

"I'll do some checking and see what I can come up with. Find out if anyone has received some money lately," Charlie said.

"Follow the money trail?" Arianna rose, needing to work out her restless energy or she wouldn't sleep when her time came.

"Charlie here worked for the FBI because of his great computer skills. He discovered information most people couldn't."

The retired FBI agent chuckled. "Yeah, one of the rare times I was in the field, I had to be rescued by this guy." He tipped his head toward Brody. "In my years of experience I've uncovered a lot of wrongdoing by following the money."

"Are you a hacker?"

Charlie burst out laughing. "I hate that word. I'm more of a persuader who entices a computer to give up its secrets. I hate secrets, and I'll work until I can undercover them."

"Don't you have to have a computer to do

that?" Arianna scanned the room and didn't see one.

"Yep, and that's why I want you to wake me up fifteen minutes earlier," Charlie peered at Brody, "so I can go get my computer. I live south, about a five-minute walk. That's how I got to know the guy who lives here. We'd keep running into each other while jogging. Willow is his sister." He downed the last of his coffee. "Brody, I found a cot in the storeroom and set it up for you. I'll take the bed since Arianna will wake me up before she needs it. Get a good night's sleep." Charlie strode toward the bedroom.

"Are you sure you want to take the first watch? You're the witness. You shouldn't take any watch."

"My life is at stake here, and I need you two rested. I'm perfectly capable of taking care of myself and even guarding you two." She balled a hand and set it on her hip. "Now go and get some sleep."

Brody rose in one fluid motion, a huge smile on his face, and closed the distance between them, stepping into her personal space. "You're quite good at taking charge."

"That's why I get paid big bucks to make decisions and assess situations."

"I had a recruiter for a big security firm who

wanted me to come work for them. The pay was twice what I made, but I decided to stay with the U.S. Marshals Service. I had come off some big cases that had gone well. I almost called the man up after my time in L.A. when that witness was killed. But I didn't want to leave the service on a black note."

"If anyone else had told me they lost a witness, I'd be worried but not with you. I've seen you on the job. So quit beating yourself up over it. Things happen that we can't control. We think we have a situation handled and then everything blows up in our face."

The smile that curved his mouth also reached deep in his brown eyes. He inched closer and with another man she would have moved back. She didn't feel the need to with Brody. She cared about him and didn't want to see him wrestling with a problem that was taken out of his hands.

His eyes softened. He cupped her face. "Most women I've dated don't understand my job. You do."

"Not even Carla?" she asked, half in jest, half in seriousness.

"You would think, but she didn't. For her, doing her job was a means to a promotion. She made it very clear she wanted to move up in the ranks. Her witnesses were just cases to her, ones she barely tolerated. When she found out

I had turned down a job that would have led to a promotion but taken me out of the field, she couldn't understand. But then I couldn't understand her attitude."

"I thought she was just mad because she was stuck in a cabin in the boonies because of me."

"She's definitely a big city gal." His hand slid around to her nape. "But I don't want to waste my time talking about her."

"No, you need to sleep because tomorrow..." Her words faded into the sudden electrifying silence, his mouth inches from her.

He didn't come any closer, but he was still close enough that she could smell the coffee he'd drunk earlier, the fresh clean scent from the soap in the shower. He would never make the final move so she wrapped her arms around him and settled her lips over his. For only a second there was a hesitation in Brody, then he took over the kiss, deepening it. He brought her up against him, so near she wondered if he could feel the pounding of her heartbeat against her rib cage.

The kiss she'd started ended all too soon when he leaned back slightly, his arms still locked around her. "We shouldn't do this. Not a good idea."

"I know. Emotions should never interfere with the case."

He nodded, laying his forehead against hers. "But it felt right. I've never had someone who got me like you do."

Her throat jammed. She felt the same way, but there was no future for them, and she didn't do casual, no matter how much he tempted her. It was going to be hard enough for her to patch her life BACK together without a broken heart. She pulled away totally.

"Go to bed. Please." There was no strength behind her words, but she needed time to compose herself, shore up her determination not to lose her heart to him. There was no way she would ask him to give up his job for her—give up everything he knew for her. She *had* to and she knew how hard that was. But if he couldn't join her, then that meant a relationship between them wouldn't stand a chance.

"Good night." He crossed to the kitchen and disappeared inside, heading for the storeroom and his cot.

Arianna sank onto the couch, her hands shaking. That trembling sensation spread throughout her body. If only they had met under different circumstances. When she scrubbed her fingertips down her face, the action reminded her of her sore and bruised skin. She pushed away all thoughts of Brody and of what was to come. After she checked her gun in her holster at her waist, she prowled the room, occasionally peeking outside from the various windows in the cabin. Nothing out of the ordinary.

For the next hour she saw the same thing when she checked out the windows. Darkness began to settle over the landscape the closer midnight came. She played back through the bits of conversation she'd had with the members of the first team for any clue that one of them was the informer.

She remembered Ted talking about his twin boys starting college in a month. Not one child but two. That was a tidy expense nowadays. Did he need extra money for his children's tuition? Then there was Dan. He liked expensive vacations. He went on and on about how he and his wife loved to travel and the places they went. How did he pay for them? She had less of a sense of Carla's tastes or expenses—almost as though she didn't have a personal life. She did notice the woman's possessions were expensive—from her shoes to her purse to her clothing. The men wouldn't have realized the money it took to buy what Carla had, but she did. She'd worked for some wealthy clients who shopped and bought the same brands that Carla had with her.

Arianna looked at her watch—ten minutes before she was to wake up Charlie—then started her last walk around the inside of the cabin. When she pushed two slats in the blinds facing the front of the place, her gaze latched on to the smoke and flames she saw in the sky.

Arianna stared for a few seconds then whirled about and raced for the storeroom to wake up Brody. There was a fire not far from the cabin to the south. Wasn't that where Charlie's house was?

EIGHT

The moment the door to the storeroom opened and light from the living room flooded inside, Brody bolted up in the cot. "Why are you waking me up? If it's time for my shift, you should be asleep." He swung his legs over the side.

"There's a fire to the south. I'm gonna wake up Charlie. It could be his place. Even if it isn't, his house could be in danger." Arianna swung around and hurried to the bedroom. She had to shake him awake.

His eyes opened, and he frowned. "It's time already?"

"There's a fire toward where you live. You need to check it out. Are there a lot of trees around your place?"

"Yes. It's mostly woods." Charlie stuck his feet into his boots then scrambled to his feet and headed for the front door to the cabin. "Stay inside. I'm going to jog a ways and see what I can discover."

Brody stood by the window from which she'd seen the fire. "Be careful. Someone might have found out you're helping us. How easy is it for someone to figure out about this place?"

"It would take some work. I didn't get to know Paul until after I retired. The same for Willow, Paul's sister." Charlie opened the door then paused. "If I can get to my house and it isn't burning, I'll bring back my computer. Forget sleep. I want to know who is behind this."

Brody shook his head. "I don't know about staying."

"Let me see what's going on before we decide."

Brody went back to the window to follow his friend's progress across the yard in the dim light of dusk.

Arianna took up guard at another window. "I agree with you. We need to leave. I discovered in my research on Rainwater that his men like using fire. It can cover up so much. I think some of Rainwater's men are getting close."

"It doesn't surprise me he has a few pyromaniacs on his payroll."

"He has a variety of different skilled murderers. I hope it wasn't Charlie's house."

Brody nodded his agreement. "I shouldn't have brought him in on this." A minute later

Brody said, "He's coming back and he doesn't have his computer."

Arianna went into the bedroom. "I'm gathering our stuff. We need to get out of here."

"Agreed." Brody opened the door before Charlie knocked. "Your place is burning?"

"Yes, the fire department is there, but I didn't let anyone know I was there. Two men stood out in the crowd gathering. They aren't my neighbors. Also as I was leaving, I saw Ted pull up."

"That was fast, even if he heard it over the radio." Brody strode to the fireplace and took the rifle down from over the mantel. "I'll make sure I get this back to Paul. We need all the firepower we can get."

"We'll go to Willow's ranch. I'm leaving my Jeep and taking Paul's old pickup truck. I think it'll get us there. Paul's been talking about selling it for scrap so there are no guarantees."

"It'll be better than your car. If they know you're helping me, then they'll be looking for your Jeep." Brody took the backpack from Arianna and slipped it over his shoulders.

Charlie went into the kitchen and came back out with a set of keys and a revolver. "I'll give this back to Paul, too. I feel naked without a weapon."

"I didn't see a truck in the shed." Arianna left the cabin sandwiched between Brody and Charlie.

"It's behind it, rusting in the elements. I think Paul would love to see it just rust to nothing."

When Arianna spotted the vehicle she could see that calling it a pickup was stretching it. "Will it work?"

"Only one way to tell." With a missing driver's door, all Charlie had to do was hop up onto the seat, stick the key in the ignition and turn it.

A cranking noise echoed through the stillness.

Arianna scanned her surroundings, imagining the loud sound alerting all Rainwater's men that they were escaping.

Charlie tried again and the engine finally turned over. "Get in. The tires are almost bare, but hopefully they'll last long enough to go ten miles to the ranch."

Brody and Arianna hurried around to the passenger side and actually had to open a door. But when she went to climb into the cab, she had to sit on the floor.

Brody crowded in after her and shut the door. "Let's go. It's probably better we're on the floor anyway."

"All I want is for this to get us to the ranch,

then it can die." Charlie pulled around the front of the shed and headed toward the road. "For this time of night, there's more traffic than usual, but then a fire does attract spectators."

"So long as they keep their focus on the fire, we can slip away." Arianna sat cross-legged facing Brody, whose back was to the dashboard, the lights on it minimal.

In the shadows she could feel Brody's gaze on her while hers fixed on him. She told herself it was because there was nowhere else to look, but that wasn't it really. There was a connection between them she couldn't deny. She needed to get through the next few days alive, testify and then leave Alaska. In her new life, she could put all of this, including Brody, behind her. She needed to quit thinking about what she wasn't going to have. Any kind of relationship beyond this was impossible.

When Charlie hit a rough patch in the road, she bounced up and forward—into Brody. He clasped her to steady her, but instead of pushing her back where she sat, he held her still for a few extra seconds, his face near hers, his breath washing over her cheek. She remembered their lives were only crossing for a short time and finally managed to pull away, planting herself as far from Brody as she could. Which wasn't nearly far enough.

"Are we almost there?" she asked Charlie, a frantic edge to her question.

"A couple more miles. Sorry about the rough ride. The shock absorbers are one of many things not working on this pickup," Charlie said.

"We'll survive," Brody said as though talking through clenched teeth. He probably was—the bouncing couldn't be doing his ankle any favors.

When Arianna studied his outline in the darkened cab, the rigid lines of his body conveyed tension.

Arianna held on to what she could when the truck went over another bumpy spot in the highway. Charlie made a sharp right turn onto a dirt road. Her grip strengthened around the bottom part of the driver's seat.

"I'm parking a ways from the house. No use for me to go nearer until closer to seven in the morning. When I leave with the trailer, I'll return to pick you two up. I don't want Willow to know anyone else is going with me. The less she's involved the better for everyone."

Brody knelt, looking around as the pickup went off the road onto an even rougher path. "Does she have hired hands who would be out at this time at night?"

"Two hands, but I doubt they'd be around.

One is her uncle and the other a friend of her deceased husband. They help her out. This is an area she doesn't use on the ranch. No cows or horses."

When Charlie stopped—or rather, when the truck spurted to a halt—Arianna opened the door, needing to get out, to breathe fresh air. Being confined so close to Brody, their legs touching, was not good for her concentration. She would check out the terrain since they would be here for six or seven hours.

For a moment she relished the cool night air, a light breeze blowing with no hint of smoke in it. An owl hooted nearby as if sending up an alarm someone was intruding. Otherwise silence reigned—except for the footsteps coming toward her.

She knew it was Brody before he stopped next to her and did his own reconnaissance of the woods cocooning them. "It's your turn to get some sleep. The bed of the truck isn't too bad. You can use the backpack as a pillow."

"What are you and Charlie gonna do?"

"Take turns keeping watch. Don't worry, we'll try and get some sleep, too."

"Where?" She didn't know if she could sleep if he lay down in the back of the pickup, too.

Brody sweep his arm across his front. "The

ground. I can sleep anywhere. Sometimes that's part of the job."

"Sleep sounds wonderful. I'm not sure I can after fleeing Paul's cabin. I should be used to not trusting anyone or anyplace, but I sure wanted to stay at his house for the night."

"Yeah, a comfortable bed is so much better than the ground or the back of a twenty-year-old pickup." Brody slipped off the backpack. "Use this if you can."

Her hand grasped the same strap he did, glancing across his knuckles. The touch only reminded her of the growing physical attraction she had for him. "Let's hope we can rest for the next six hours and not have to escape. I don't know if that truck can go another foot."

Brody chuckled. "It did sound like it died for good. Let's hope we don't have to find out. Surely our transportation in the morning will be better."

Sitting on an aluminum floor in a horse trailer was a step up from sitting on the floor in Paul's pickup, but Arianna hated not being able to see outside without standing up.

"The scenery is beautiful along this highway. You'll get glimpses of it through the windows." Brody took a place next to her at the front of the two-horse trailer. "It looks like we'll have hours to kill."

"Please, not that word." Arianna retied her hair into a ponytail, strands of it whipping about her in the cool breeze coming in from the partially open windows. "I'm glad we'll have pretty good cell reception along most of the trip. I want to be forewarned if there's a roadblock."

"The good thing about going this way instead of the Parks Highway is that there's less traffic."

"Yeah, but longer timewise. At least this mode of transportation isn't obvious."

"And there's an area you can hide in the storage part for the tack."

Arianna peered up at a mare looking at her with her big brown eyes. "When I was a girl, I rode all the time. I wanted to raise horses. I wish I could have talked with Willow instead of having to sneak into the trailer." Brody started to say something, but she held up her hand. "I know, the less people know what we are doing the better."

"Why did you like to ride horses?"

"Are you kidding? Most little girls at some time in their lives think about having their own horse. At least my friends and I did. But mostly I did because my dad loved to ride and it was a way for me to connect with him. We used to ride when he was home several times a week until I left for college. Now it doesn't make any difference."

"Was he gone a lot?"

Thinking about her father and the angry words they'd exchanged over her leaving the army closed her throat. When Brody looked at her, waiting for an answer, she swallowed several times and said, "He was always gone on some kind of mission. He was up for general and didn't get it the last time I saw him at Christmas. I've always wondered if what happened to me was the reason why. He certainly had done everything he could to get it."

"Have you talked with your dad about what happened? Explained your reasons?"

"I tried when I first came home. He didn't want to hear it." The kindness in Brody's eyes urged her to tell him everything. "What if I— died and my father and I never make things right? He would blame himself. Not right away but in the end."

"I can carry a message to him if you want."

A lump the size of Alaska lodged in her throat. She couldn't get a word out. All she could do was nod, tears shimmering in her eyes. She didn't cry. What good would it do her to bemoan her predicament? It wouldn't change anything. *Trust the Lord.* She needed to keep that in the foreground. But no matter what she told herself, a tear slipped down her face.

He caressed his thumb across the top of her cheek. "Don't think about it now. Let's get through the trial. I'll help you any way I can. It won't be easy, but you're tough or you wouldn't do what you've been doing. You survived someone trying to frame you. You've protected many others who needed your services and you didn't lose anyone." His voice caught on the last part of that sentence.

"Tell me what happened when you lost your witness."

"I was waiting at the courthouse, coordinating the security there when the car transporting the witness was ambushed. A marshal and the witness were killed and two marshals were wounded. It was a fast and brutal attack. Later we discovered the cell phone on the witness that led the assailants to his location."

She took his hand and held it. "I'm so sorry. At least I knew better than to bring along a cell phone."

"But not your gun or knife."

"That's different, and I needed them so it was a good thing that I had them."

Brody's eyes clouded. "Yeah, you did need them. You shouldn't have."

"In a perfect world. This isn't a perfect world."

She squeezed his hand gently. "And you remember that. You told the man what he had to do, and he didn't follow directions. Remember, we can't control everything. I'm really discovering that lately."

"Yes, but the consequences affected so many. The families of the marshal killed and the families of the criminal's next victims. Without the witness's testimony, he was acquitted and within a year killed two more. One was a mother with two young children. I'll never forget seeing those kids at her funeral. They haunt my dreams."

"You didn't kill their mother. You can't think like that." Hearing the anguish in his voice made her want to forget what was happening and just comfort him.

"I have a hard time forgiving myself."

"And I have a hard time forgiving Dirk for what he did. What a pair we are. It's not easy to move on with that kind of baggage." She grasped his upper arm, trying to impart her support.

"I try not to think about it. I guess seeing Carla again brought it all back."

"You need to deal with it, not avoid it. Was the guy convicted when he killed those two other people?"

"Yes, I'm happy to say he'll be in prison for the rest of his life, but—"

She put her fingers over his mouth. "No buts. They aren't allowed. These past two months have given me a lot of time to think about my past. I've let Dirk's betrayal rule my life for the past four years. It possibly colored how I dealt with my dad's disapproval. I got defensive. Now I can't do anything about it. It was bad enough what Dirk did to me, but it's worse that I'm still letting him affect me. When this is all over, I intend to put the man in the past where he belongs. If that means I forgive him, then I'll find a way. I'll have enough to deal with trying to piece together some kind of life." *Without anyone I know. I'll be totally alone.*

"That part of being a U.S. marshal never appealed to me. My life may be a mess, but I can't imagine giving up everything and starting new."

His words only confirmed what she'd thought, and that no matter how much she was starting to care about him it would go nowhere. Arianna pushed to her feet, holding on to the side to keep herself balanced while the trailer was speeding down the highway. Pretending an interest in the mare nearest her, she stroked the horse's nose—anything to keep from looking at him. She was afraid she would start crying if she thought about how she was feeling and what her future would be.

"I'm sorry. I shouldn't have said that. You don't need to hear that now."

A band about her chest constricted her. She needed to say something to him, but she couldn't. Why did she meet a man she was attracted to when there was nothing that she could do about it? It wasn't fair, but then having to go into the Witness Protection Program was unfair.

Life isn't always fair. Do the best you can with what you're given.

Her grandma's advice slinked into her mind and began to ease some of the tightness in her chest. She inhaled a deep, soothing breath and said, "Yes, I do. You're right."

"I—" The throwaway cell rang, and Brody answered it. "I think that's a good idea. I'm starved." When he hung up, he rose and came toward Arianna. "Charlie is pulling into a place he knows up the road to get something for us to eat. They have restrooms on the outside of the building, so he'll park near them. That way we can sneak and use them without anyone spotting us."

"Good. I could use walking around a little. I was getting stiff sitting." She'd started to feel confined, something she felt when she thought about her future. She still didn't know what she was going to do.

As the trailer slowed down and Charlie pulled off the highway, Arianna patted the mare's neck, wishing she could get on her and ride away.

The driver's door slammed shut then Charlie slapped the side of the van. "We're here, and it's all clear. I'll be inside getting us something to eat. When we leave, I'll top off the tank. Don't know when we can stop next."

Brody peered out at the gas station/convenience store. "Let's go. I see another car pulling in for gas."

Exiting the side door of the trailer, she hurried toward the restroom. The length of the horse trailer and large pickup blocked her from anyone seeing her from the store or in front of it pumping gas. Brody was right behind her, moving quickly.

A few minutes later as she washed her hands and wiped a wet towel over her face, the sound of a knock made her stiffen. She swung around, staring at the door. Under her light jacket she had her gun. Her pulse rate jumped as she put her hand on her Glock and moved forward. "It's being used."

"Oh, sorry. I'll pay for the gas then come back."

Arianna went to the door and listened for the

crunch of the pebbles layering the ground outside that indicated the woman walked away. When she heard it, she relaxed her tense shoulders. Waiting ten more seconds, she eased the door open and peeked out. Clear.

She rushed toward the horse van at the same time a man came around the end of the trailer. She halted as though caught doing something wrong. Making sure her gun wasn't visible, she pulled her jacket around, crossing her arms at her waist.

"Beautiful day," she murmured and continued her trek toward the pickup as though she was getting into the cab.

When the man entered the restroom, she rushed to the side door of the trailer and inched it open slowly, hoping the hinges didn't squeak too loud. The noise of the men's restroom door being unlocked spurred her to move faster. She clambered into the horse trailer, shutting herself inside and ducking down at the back. She prayed the man didn't check out the horses by looking into any of the windows. But the sound of his footsteps faded around the back of the trailer. She slumped against the side.

Where's Brody? If the restroom was free for the stranger, then he should have been in here. The urge to search for him tested her. She shouldn't. Not yet. But she didn't want anything to happen to him because of her. That she couldn't deal with—not with all the deaths so far associated with Rainwater murdering Thomas Perkins.

The side door open. Arianna drew her gun and brought it up as Brody said, "It's me."

She sighed and laid her hand holding the gun in her lap. A tiny voice in her head told her to wait to put it back in her holster. What if someone was with him, forcing him to reveal her?

But when he appeared in the entrance, he was alone. His gaze lit upon her Glock. "Were there any problems?" He shut the door.

"Where were you?"

"I went to the restroom."

"After that. A man came around to go in there and it was free. I thought you would be in the trailer. You weren't." Her voice rose with frustration and strain. *I want my life back.*

"Did he say anything to you or indicate he knew you?" Brody sat next to her, his left side touching her right one.

"No. His body language seemed okay, too. Nothing to alarm me. So where were you?"

"I saw a black SUV similar to the one that dropped Carla off yesterday. It stopped at the pump and the driver got some gas. He wasn't familiar, but I couldn't see if there was anyone else inside the car. I sneaked around the other side to get a better look. Once the SUV left, I hightailed it back here."

"So nothing suspicious?" Arianna whispered, aware their normal voices could carry beyond the back of the trailer.

"I didn't say that." Brody leaned close to her and lowered his voice even more. "I got the gut feeling there was someone else in the car. He kept looking at the passenger side when he was checking out the area around him. There was nothing casual about him. Vigilant. On edge."

"When he looked over here, did he react differently?"

"I couldn't tell. He was turned from me."

"I hope—" The sound of someone outside the horse trailer made her swallow the rest of her words.

"It's me," Charlie said before opening the side door. "Got you each a turkey and Swiss sandwich, a bag of chips and because I'm so nice a chocolate chip cookie." He glanced from side to side then continued. "There's talk of a roadblock on Glenn Allen Highway so we're going to Valdez and taking the ferry to Anchorage. We'll get into Anchorage after dark. That might not be so bad."

A few minutes later, Charlie had them back on the highway heading south.

Being so close to Brody wasn't safe for her

peace of mind. She wanted to know everything about him and that was dangerous. The more she discovered the more she liked him. "I'm getting sore sitting on this hard surface. I wonder if I can do some yoga stretches, maybe work some of the stiffness out of my body." She scooted a few feet from him.

"Are you one of those people who can't rest even when you get the chance?"

"That about sums me up. I need to be kept busy but occasionally I do stop to play Scrabble or read a good book." She snapped her fingers. "I don't seem to have one with me."

"I should have had Charlie stop at the library on the way out of Fairbanks. Oh, yeah. He couldn't since we left before any library would be open."

"It wouldn't be a bad idea for you to do some of these exercises with me. Nothing where we stand up and balance ourselves. I don't think going sixty miles an hour is conducive to that."

He twisted around and sank down, laying his head on the backpack. "Wake me if we're in trouble."

"I doubt seriously you'll be able to sleep through it. The sound of my gun going off in here will probably start a two horse stampede."

"So long as they go out the door and not back here." Brody closed his eyes.

Arianna sat cross-legged with her spine straight and the back of her hands lying on her knees. Washing her mind of all concerns, she let a calmness flow through her. From there she moved into a core pose, then a back bend followed by an inversion, throwing her legs over her head. The stretches felt great, removing her from all that had happened to her.

The cell rang. Brody popped up, digging for it in his pocket. "Yes?"

He listened, a frown curving deep lines into his face. When he hung up he said, "That black SUV is stalled up ahead. A woman, not Carla according to Charlie's description, is waving us down. He's going to blow by them."

The speed of the horse trailer picked up. Charlie swerved into the other lane and increased their pace even more. Brody knelt on the side they would pass the SUV and peeked out the window. He dropped down and went for his gun. "Two more men are getting out, both with big guns."

NINE

"Get back against the wall." Brody cocooned Arianna's body between him and the aluminum wall.

"Don't. Flatten yourself next to me." She tried to push him away.

"No." He poured all the authority he could into that one word. She was not going to die here on the road.

Shots blasted the air. Suddenly the trailer swerved toward the side of the highway where the SUV probably was. The speed of the trailer decreased. He dragged Arianna to the floor and covered her again.

"What's—"

The loud sounds of the crash reverberated through the trailer. The hard impact of it crashing into the SUV jolted him, and although he knew what Charlie had decided to do, he wasn't able to keep himself from being thrown off Arianna, sliding toward the back door. All around him, he could hear the hooves of the panicked horses as they stamped the floor and tried to stay on their feet.

When he looked back toward Arianna to make sure she was okay, her body rammed against his at the same time the mare brought a hoof down toward her head.

Arianna saw the hoof coming toward her and flinched away from it so that it only clipped her left shoulder. Pain bolted through her.

She looked toward Brody. The other mare crashed to the floor, not able to remain standing. Her eyes wide, the horse tried to get up, but the trailer was swinging around toward the truck. Coming to a stop, the trailer tilted at an angle as though hanging over a cliff. The area they'd been driving through was relatively flat. A ditch?

A woman's scream pierced the air. Shots sounded again, this time from a different gun.

Charlie's? Arianna got up on her knees and hands. "Okay?"

"Yes." Brody's gaze was riveted to the mare still on her feet, dancing about and tugging on her tethers. He rose, searching for his gun that had been knocked from his hand. "Calm her if you can."

As he struggled up the inclined floor toward the front of the trailer, Arianna gripped one of the mare's ropes and yanked her as far away as she could from the horse still lying on its side, her legs flailing. The downed animal's body banged against the side of the trailer, her head whipped back and forth against her restraints. The panicked horses' guttural cries ripped at Arianna's heart.

She looked out the window near her. They were teetering over a drop-off along the side of the road. The mare she held would counter the other's weight and help keep them from sliding down into the ditch. She stretched to see the bottom of the gully. She could see it, maybe eight feet down. She pulled even more to coax the mare the few remaining feet to the tack area at the front.

She would secure the mare to a bar, then follow Brody outside. She wouldn't stay in the trailer while there were at least three assailants. She hated leaving the frightened horses in the trailer but the only way out for them was through the back doors, which opened into the ditch.

Another round of gunfire pushed her faster. Charlie could really be hurt. The front of the truck he was driving took most of the impact with the SUV. As Arianna made her way to the small side door, the mare yanked on the rope. Her last glance back at the horse showed an animal with wide eyes, trying desperately to get loose. The one in the back of the trailer struggled to her feet, the rope tied to her halter still connected to the trailer.

Lord, watch over them. Us.

Arianna eased the side door open, her gun drawn, a bullet in the chamber.

On the ground lay one assailant, not moving, a bullet hole in his chest.

She checked his pulse then sneaked forward toward the cab of the truck. Where was Brody?

A noise on the other side drew her full attention. Glancing over the hitch that connected the horse trailer to the truck, she spied Brody struggling with another man. To the side of her, she heard a door creaking open. She turned toward that nearer and more immediate threat as Charlie tumbled out of the cab, blood running down his face.

Brody's attacker broke free of him and tried to run toward the SUV. Brody leaped forward and drove the man to the ground inches from the drop-off. The guy heaved up and rolled over, sending Brody and him into the gully. Rocks and vegetation stabbed him on his trek down. He landed in a couple of inches of runoff with his assailant on top of him, the air swooshing from his lungs, his face pressed into the water.

Margaret Daley 181

He had to take care of his assailant and protect Arianna.

With his face still in the few inches of water, Brody struggled to turn his head so he could breathe. His thoughts clouded from lack of oxygen. He felt his attacker's hot breath on his neck. Through the haze in his mind an idea came to him. With all his energy he used his head as a sledgehammer striking the man on him in the face. Momentarily his assailant let up, drawing back slightly. A howl of rage pierced the air.

Adrenaline zipped through Brody. Putting all his energy into hoisting himself up and throwing off his opponent, he thought of Arianna alone in an unfamiliar place with no way to get to Anchorage. He would not let that happen, which meant he couldn't die here today. He tossed the man off him and turned around, scrambling to his feet at the same time his attacker did. The man drew a knife, flicking it open. The eyes of the man were full of determination to kill him. Brody moved in a slow circle, scouring the area for any kind of weapon. There was none.

As Charlie sank to his knees, Arianna rushed to him. "Are you hit?"

He shook his head, drops of blood spattering onto the side of the road. "The windshield is shattered from the bullets. Probably a few fragments cut my face. It happened so fast. I'm fine." He started to stand but collapsed back down.

Arianna examined him. "I think you were grazed by a bullet."

"Could be. I aimed the truck at the SUV and the gunmen. I ducked as they sprayed the pickup."

"Stay put." She went to the opened door of the truck and searched for Charlie's gun. When she found it, she took it to him and put it in his hand. "I'm checking the area. Brody was wrestling one on the other side. One is on the ground. Where's the woman?"

"Don't know. I tried to return fire, but I must have lost consciousness briefly."

Arianna slowly rotated in a circle to check around her. Other than the dead body a few yards away, she didn't see anyone else on this side. With her gun in hand, she crept forward to round the front of the SUV. The truck had smashed into its side, T-boning it. That was when she saw another man pinned between the pickup and the SUV. His assault rifle was still clutched in his hand but there was no life in his shocked eyes. Arianna felt for a pulse just in case but found none. So at least three men and a woman.

Rainwater has to be stopped. Death follows him around.

Anger surged to the foreground, firming her resolve to make it alive to the trial to testify. No man should be above the law.

When she rounded the SUV, a woman flew at her, tackling Arianna to the hard ground.

Poised on the balls of his feet, Brody was ready to dodge the medium-built man. Every nerve alert, he tingled with anticipation of the attack to come. He smelled of mud, brackish water and sweat. The sun beat down on Brody, but a chill gripped him.

His gaze glued on his attacker, he waited for the move. Speed would be paramount. The man charged him, the knife pointed at Brody's heart. With his booted feet, he lashed out at the assailant's legs at the same time he grabbed for the guy's wrist. The assailant twisted his arm away. Brody pounded his right fist into the man's jaw while kicking him again.

The attacker fell to his knees, the knife dropping from his hand. Brody moved in and hit him in the face several times until the man crashed forward into the water. Gasping for air, Brody snatched up the knife, then rolled the assailant over. The man was out cold.

Brody removed the guy's belt and secured

his hands behind him. He had to make sure there weren't any others on Rainwater's payroll around. He clambered up the incline to clear the scene and to find his gun and something better to tie up his assailant.

As her attacker went for Arianna's neck, choking her, she looked into the woman's crazed eyes.

"You killed him," the lady shouted over and over.

Gripping her wrists to pry her hands from around her neck, Arianna twisted and bucked, trying to knock the woman off her. Her oxygen-starved lungs screamed for air. A haze descended over her mind.

Suddenly her assailant was lifted from Arianna, and she gulped in precious breaths until the feeling of light-headedness faded.

Brody held the kicking and screeching woman against him. "Okay?"

Arianna nodded, grabbed her gun from the ground a couple of feet away and rose, her legs shaky for a few seconds. "I'll take care of her. Secure the crime scene. Charlie is—"

"Right here. I've called a highway patrol officer I'm good friends with. We can trust him. Someone will have to clean up this mess. A trucker is coming. We're going to have to do some fast-talking if we intend to get away before this place is mobbed. I figure we'll need to use your badge."

Brody looked toward the road. "Take care of the guy in the ditch. I'll take care of the people who want to help until your friend gets here. Arianna, get some rope from the trailer to tie up both of our attackers. Make sure the horses are still okay."

Images of this incident on Richardson Highway being splashed all over the news spurred her to move as fast as her sore body allowed. They had to contain this until they could get away or Rainwater's men would know exactly where she was.

"The trooper I left at the wreck owes me. He'll process the scene as slowly as he can, especially when it comes to notifying people about what happened on Richardson Highway. The two dead men will be picked up and the other two will end up going to headquarters since their injuries are minor. Johnson will tell the commander to check with the U.S. Marshals Service, but he'll delay that as long as possible."

"Thanks, Gus," Charlie said in the front seat of the state trooper's car, speeding back toward Fairbanks. "We need to be as far away from this as possible before Rainwater's men discover the way we're heading to get to Anchorage. They'll have those routes locked up tighter than an oil drum."

Gus chuckled. "Won't they be surprised when you aren't going that way."

Brody glanced toward Arianna sitting across from him in the rear seat in the vehicle. Her head rested on the back cushion, her eyes closed. "Who's this pilot that can fly us to Seward?"

"A childhood friend. He had a run-in with Rainwater's smuggling operations once when he was flying up north to St. Lawrence Island. He barely made it out alive. Believe me there was no love lost between them, but I didn't tell him who you are. Just to keep this quiet. There'll be a car waiting for you at the airstrip in Seward. Another trooper who I know isn't on anyone's payroll other than the state's arranged it. He doesn't know why I asked."

Brody had known from the beginning when they were running away from the cabin that he'd have to trust a few people to help him and Arianna get to the courthouse in Anchorage. But the more people they brought into the circle the more the chances increased that Rainwater's men could discover their whereabouts. That was not an option. At least he was the only one who knew where they would stay in Anchorage—if they could get there.

"While you were securing the two prisoners in the back of the trooper's car, I placed a call to Willow. She's heading toward the wreck site to pick up her horses. I was so glad I could reassure her that neither one was injured badly—just shook up and with a few minor cuts. I'm really going to have to make this up to her."

"Was she mad at you?" Brody asked, remembering leading the horses out of the trailer right before the second state trooper showed up. One limped from a cut on her leg, but otherwise the mare appeared all right and calm once out of the trailer. He sure hoped there were no lasting effects to the animals.

Angling toward Brody, Charlie grinned. "No. She was more concerned about my injuries. I'm definitely going to have to take the woman out to dinner when this all settles down."

"She's a keeper, my friend." Brody looked toward Arianna again, relieved she wasn't injured. Her soft gaze trained on him lured him toward her. "Okay?"

Her eyes gleamed. "I'm relishing the calm while I have it. We both know how quickly that can change. One minute we're just riding along and the next we're ramming a car."

"Don't worry about that," Gus interjected. "We're almost to my friend's place. You'll be safe."

Her eyebrows rose, and she mouthed the word "safe," as though in her world that wasn't possible.

Which Brody could see. They both were used to guarding people in trouble. What would it be like to not do something like that? To wake up each morning not worried about a security plan or if he had all the options covered?

Arianna fully faced him on the seat and said in a soft voice, "We left a mess back there."

"Once you've testified I can straighten everything out."

"I hope I can tomorrow. The prosecutor has only one witness left, according to Gus. That'll be cutting it close."

"But better in the long run. I'll only have to keep you hidden in Anchorage overnight. Less time for Rainwater's men to find us."

"Once I've given my testimony the easy part is over with."

"This is easy? What kind of life do you normally lead?" he said with a laugh, trying to coax a smile from her. He knew exactly what she was referring to and to him the aftermath of the trial would be the hardest part of all of this—reinventing yourself.

"One I'm not sure how to let go. When you're used to a certain kind of challenge and excitement, how do you live without it?"

"Get excited about something else? Don't let the circumstances you can't control pull you down?"

She did smile then. "Both good suggestions."

He bent closer to her and whispered, "Don't forget tonight to write that letter to your parents. I'll see they get it."

"But I can't get a response from them. What if I refuse being in WitSec?"

"You put yourself and anyone around you in danger. They would use your family to get to you. They know that when a person goes into the program, all contact is lost so there is no reason to use your family like that. It has to be that way for yours and others' safety."

She sighed and closed her eyes for a few seconds. When she reconnected with him visually, there was a sheen to the gray depths, like light shining on silver. "I know. I would never put someone I love in danger."

A tall, redheaded man stood by a twin-engine plane at the end of a flat, grassy field. Gus slowed his car to a stop next to his childhood friend. "Hal thought this would be a better place to take off from than an airport—even a private one. He uses this field sometimes. It's not far from his property."

Arianna started to open her door, but Brody caught her hand on the seat between them and held it for a second. "Ready?"

"Yes," she murmured, then slipped from his grasp and pushed the door open.

No matter how tough Arianna was, this past forty-eight hours had taken its toll on her. She tried to put up a brave front, but occasionally when she didn't think he was looking, he saw the sadness in her eyes. It ate at him. This wasn't fair. She was doing the right thing by testifying against Rainwater, and yet she would pay the price as much as the crime boss. She was losing her family, her career, everything she knew and was special to her. Anger knotted his stomach. He shoved open his door and climbed from the car.

The next twenty hours would be the hardest of the trip. He figured that Rainwater had a chokehold around all the ways into Anchorage with spies everywhere.

Within ten minutes Gus's friend took off with Brody in the backseat next to Arianna. She stared out the window, silent since getting out of the car. While Charlie carried on a conversation with Hal, Brody studied Arianna's stiff posture, the tensing of her jaw as if she gritted her teeth. He wanted to comfort her with more than words. He wanted to hold her tight against him. He wanted to kiss her again.

The revelation made him frown. He cared for her and that wasn't smart at all. Although Carla had been a marshal, not a witness, he'd mixed his professional life with his personal one and that had ended badly. It was especially unwise to become involved with a witness. After his work was done, she would be whisked away. He would never see her again.

He swung his attention to the side window next to him and stared at the ground below. Mountainous terrain spread in all directions. Patches of snow on the peaks. Blue lakes. Green forests. Beautiful.

"Nearer to Seward, I'm flying under the radar. I'm going out over the water and coming in from that direction," Hal announced, pointing due south. "It'll take us a little longer, but I think that will be the best approach to the airstrip. If anything happens and we go down in the water, there are life preservers under your seats."

Arianna looked at Brody. "I always laugh when the flight attendants on the airlines go through the procedure for water landings when we're only going over land. I know it's some regulation that they must follow no matter what. But in this case, we may need to know the information."

"Don't worry about it. We won't go down. But if we do, the life preserver will hold you up until—"

As she held up her hand to stop him talking, a smile danced in her eyes. "I'm not concerned. It isn't rushing water. When this is over with and I get wherever I'm to live, I'm going to take swimming lessons. Dog-paddling isn't dignified. I should be able to do better than that. It's about time I conquer a childhood fear."

"Is that a challenge for me to conquer mine?"

"Not with me. Only with yourself. I'll never know if you conquered it or not," she said in a detached voice, then returned her attention to looking out the window.

His throat closed. He clenched his jaws so tight that dull pain streaked down his neck. He wanted something different for Arianna, for both of them, but her fate was sealed when she'd witnessed Thomas Perkins's murder. He was thankful she believed in the Lord. He would be with her and give her the added strength she would need to start over.

"Do you know of a helicopter company with the letters CAR?" Brody asked the pilot, wanting to concentrate on the present—not the future.

"The only one I can think of is a small outfit

called Carson Transportation. Why do you want to know about them?"

"We saw them flying over the fire area."

"They fly tourists and sometimes reporters to different places around here. They have a good reputation in Fairbanks."

Arianna looked at Brody. "So it might have been innocent."

"Maybe. Or maybe they didn't know who they were dealing with."

Nearing land, Hal turned toward the north. Brody spied the runway up ahead, not long enough for large airplanes. The next few hours would be dicey. *Lord, we need all Your help. People like Rainwater shouldn't get away with murder.*

Arianna clutched the edge of her seat as the plane touched down, only releasing her grip as Hal taxied toward the small terminal.

When Brody climbed from the plane, he offered Arianna his hand, not sure she would take it. But she did. The feel of it in his caused him to thank the Lord for getting them this far.

Charlie joined them. "Gus said a white Chevy would be parked in the lot near the main building."

At the car, Charlie searched under the back tire on the driver's side. Rising, he held up a set of keys. Both Brody and Arianna slipped into the backseat while Charlie settled behind the steering wheel and started the engine.

As Charlie pulled out onto Airport Road, Brody said, "We need to get a change of clothing. If those two back at the wreck have been interviewed, Rainwater's men may know what we're wearing and how we're disguised."

"Good point. I know just the place. I've been to Seward a couple of times so far this year. Besides, this is tourist season and everything is in full swing."

"I suggest we also find a place with makeup. I've been thinking we should age ourselves. It might help," Arianna said.

"Have you had any experience in doing that?" Brody asked as he kept his attention trained on what was going on around them. He felt Arianna's presence next to him deep down—an awareness that went beyond the visual. He could be in a totally dark room and know she was there. Maybe it was her scent, but something he couldn't explain linked him to her.

"Yes, two years in high school and one in college. I loved working behind the scenes in stage productions."

Surprised by this new bit of information, Brody briefly skimmed his gaze over her before returning to his vigil. "I never would have thought you'd do that."

Her chuckle peppered the air. "You probably envisioned me as a tomboy growing up."

"You do have three brothers, and you're the only girl in a family steeped in the military."

"My mother and grandma, true Southern belles, had a strong influence on me. I liked girly things."

"And yet you went into the army."

"Warrior by day and diva by night."

"That I'd like to see. Wait, I've seen the warrior part."

Arianna laughed again. "Then I'll give you an aging diva. That ought to throw people off."

Later when Brody escorted her to the Chevy, Arianna felt like a new person in a flowered dress with added padding in a couple of places to give the appearance of an extra thirty pounds. Heavy makeup had changed her with a few age spots on her face as well as wrinkles. Wearing a wig of gray hair, she'd aged herself by forty years. She curved her shoulders to give the effect she was humped over and used a cane. Her shuffling gait carried her slowly to the car. She waited until Brody opened the door.

Once everyone was back in the car—a Chevy with Aurora Tours painted in black on the sides—she admired the look that Brody had come up with. He wore a ball cap with blond hair sticking out, hiding his dark color beneath. He'd sculpted a big belly that flowed over his belt. Wearing a light jacket, black shorts with white socks almost up to his knees and sandals, he looked the image of a tourist who hadn't read about the cooler temperatures in Alaska even though it was the end of July.

"Now all I have to do is touch up your face a little." Arianna opened the bag with her jars, tubes and brushes. "This makes me feel like I'm back in high school, but I'm the drama teacher."

Charlie rotated around, wearing a gray wig, too, and a long moustache. His attire was similar to Brody's. "Ready to go. There shouldn't be any roadblocks—at least from law enforcement. Good thing you thought to have Gus get the higher-ups to call off looking for Arianna with roadblocks."

"So if we see one, we'll know they're Rainwater's men. I doubt they would do that so close to Anchorage. Too easy for the real state troopers to come upon them." Brody closed his eyes as she put light color foundation around them.

"But they'll have lookouts watching all the ways into Anchorage." Arianna darkened the skin under his eyes to give him circles, then shaded his nose to make it more prominent.

"Yeah, we can't act suspicious either," Charlie said from the front seat.

When she finished the makeup job on Brody, she inspected her work. "You look good for an old man."

He patted his fake large stomach. "One who is definitely out of shape. Won't be able to run a hundred-meter race in ten seconds."

She whistled. "That's great for an amateur."

Brody puffed out his chest, which looked funny with the belly. "I'll have you know I was on the track team in high school and college."

"So while I was a drama geek, you were a track star."

"I won't say the star, but I did pretty good." His gaze brushed over her. "And I can't imagine you being a geek anytime."

"Oh, but I was. We moved so much I never felt I fit in anywhere. I was quite shy in high school. Being in drama allowed me to make up characters and become them. I even toyed with being a drama teacher once. Briefly."

"What changed your mind?"

"A Jackson serves his, or in my case, her country. That is the tradition. Even my mother was a nurse in the army when she met my dad."

As Charlie left Seward, he increased his speed. Arianna relaxed to enjoy the scenery. This area had been on her list of places to explore after her job two months ago ended. Seward Highway was a scenic road meant to be taken slow with many stops to see what Alaska had to offer. But she hoped they didn't stop at all. She would breathe easier when she was in the safe house in Anchorage—at least until tomorrow when they would leave for the courthouse.

I'm in Your hands, Lord. I know You're with me.

Those thoughts gave her comfort. She'd done all she could—prepare and pray.

As Charlie drove through a pass, mountains surrounded them, hemming them in, while steel-blue lakes dotted the terrain. In the sky an eagle soared near the water's edge. Beautiful. Tranquil. She shoved down the yearning to spend time here. That could never be.

Charlie decreased his speed. Arianna looked out the windshield as the traffic got thicker and slower.

"I think there's a wreck up ahead," Charlie said in a tight voice. "I don't like it one bit."

In another half-mile, the stream of cars came to a standstill. Brody leaned forward. "It looks like a semi on its side. That's going to block traffic for a while."

"I feel like a duck sitting on a lake surrounded

by hunters waiting for duck season to open," Charlie said.

Charlie's image said it all. "That is what we are," Arianna said, scanning the area and cars parked around them. People began getting out, talking to their neighbors stranded on the highway with them.

Charlie drummed his hand against the steering wheel as more people poured out of their vehicles. "It's going to look strange if you don't get out, stretch and view the magnificent scenery."

A frown carved more lines into Brody's face. "I know. Let's give it a little time. Maybe they'll move the truck soon."

Charlie craned his neck. "I think I see two down and this couldn't have happened more than fifteen or twenty minutes ago because we're close enough to see the wreck. This is tourist season so the traffic is thicker at this time."

"Great. I don't want us to stay out too long. If we do, we need to minimize our interaction with others."

Arianna peered at the groups of people forming, talking. A couple of people opened the trunks of their vehicles and dug into a cooler then began passing around drinks. "This may turn into one big party. I think we need to mingle with the crowd. Few are staying in their cars."

"You two mingle. I'll stand back and watch. That'll fit with my role as tour guide," Charlie said.

Arianna turned to Brody. "We'll be Ethel and Bob Manley in Alaska for the first time."

"You're enjoying this," Brody said, his frown deepening.

"No, but we can make the best of this situation. Our disguises are good. We just have to act the part of an older couple who have been married for forty years."

"Where are we from? You've got everything else figured out," he said with a smirk.

She playfully hit his arm. "Don't be a grouch." Snapping her fingers, she smiled. "Better yet, be an old grouch. A good role for you. I've dragged you to Alaska, and you didn't want to come. We live in Florida. You're rather be on a beach."

"Anything else?"

"No, just go with the flow. And keep things simple."

"Yes, Ethel."

Charlie left the car and opened the door for Arianna.

When Brody rounded the back of the car, she took his arm and strolled toward the side of the road, "Isn't this beautiful? A lot better than a hot sandy beach."

"No," he grumbled. "I'm too cold. They should plaster all over those tourist brochures how cold it is here."

"It's not cold, Bob. I told you shorts weren't needed. Besides, you have such bony knees."

Brody stopped and stared down at his legs. "I do not."

Arianna patted his arm. "Dear, let's not argue. It's a gorgeous day." Not far from another couple, probably in their forties, she gave them a smile. "Are you two from Alaska?"

"No, visiting like you. We couldn't help overhearing." The blond-haired woman stuck her hand out. "I'm Laura and this is my husband, Terry."

After they exchanged handshakes, Terry asked, "Did you take a cruise here? We just got off a ship. We'll be flying out of Anchorage in a few days after we see this place."

Brody rocked back and forth on his feet. "Nope. Get seasick. I put my foot down when Ethel wanted to take a cruise to Alaska. We settled on flying here. We're leaving Anchorage next week."

"What are y'all doing?" Laura asked, looking Arianna up and down as though checking her out. The couple seemed harmless, but she knew this could turn into a dangerous situation if they let their guard down. She'd seen it in the Middle East with suicide bombers.

"Seeing the countryside. A couple days ago we went to Denali National Park so today we went down to Seward. On our way back to Anchorage." She leaned more on her cane. "All this walking is taking a toll on my knees."

"What did you like the best about Denali? We're going there tomorrow." Laura stuck her hands in the deep pockets of her light jacket.

Exhausted, Arianna searched her mind for what she read about the park. Bits and pieces of information about Denali materialized, but her attention strayed when a large man approached through the crowd and paused nearby, close enough to hear what she said.

Brody tossed his head toward Charlie leaning against the car. "Our guide over there drove us to Savage River Trailhead. Got to see a great view of Mount McKinley. We took a bus tour from there because the rest of the roads aren't accessible for private cars. We saw moose, lots of birds, caribou, fox and wolves."

"Don't forget the grizzly we saw from the bus. Good thing we were inside and he was outside." Arianna fanned herself. "Wow, that got my heart pumping." She watched the muscular man in jeans, cowboy boots and plaid shirt move farther away and plant himself near another group of people talking. She released a breath slowly. "I'd just as soon see a grizzly in the zoo, not the wild. Huge. She had two cubs with her. I heard they are ferocious about protecting their young. Aren't they, Bob?" She elbowed him in the rib.

He'd been staring into the crowd with the man. "Uh-huh. Sorry, sweet pea. Looking around at this place. You reckon we're gonna be here long? I could use a nap."

Terry nodded. "I could, too. I'm on vacation. A nap is a requirement." He peered toward the wreck blocking the highway. "Looks like the state troopers are here and some kind of big tow truck to get the semis moved."

"Honeybun, I need to sit down. My knees are starting to hurt being on my feet for so long today. Nice to meet you two." Arianna gave each one a smile then hobbled toward the Chevy with Brody trailing her.

Even with her head down, she slanted a glance around. Another man halted next to the muscular one who had stopped near them and said something to him. Both men hurried away.

Charlie opened the back door for her, and she eased onto the seat like she was seventy years old, putting the cane in front of her and holding its knob at the end while Brody and Charlie pretended to be in a deep conversation about where to go when they got to Anchorage—loud enough that people could easily hear.

Another lone man strolled not far from them, checking something on his cell. A photo of one of them? Arianna grinned at him then purposely looked away as if she had not a care in the world. But she noticed that Brody kept track of him, a hard glint in his eyes.

When a cheer went up a few hundred feet nearer the wreck, Arianna struggled to stand slowly although she had so much energy from the adrenaline in her body she could dance a jig for the crowd's entertainment. The back end of one semi was being moved to the side of the road.

"About time," Charlie mumbled, his mouth pinched in a frown. "I've seen at least three or four suspicious persons inspecting the people in and out of their cars."

Everyone watched the second semi being towed away and clapped. Arianna sat again, and this time closed the car door. Tension vibrated through her. She should be used to this kind of stress. It was her job. But she cared too much for Brody, even Charlie. She didn't want anything to happen to them because of her.

Charlie slid into the front seat while Brody

climbed in next to her. Charlie started the car. Brody exhaled and lounged back.

A loud crack boomed.

TEN

Brody pushed Arianna down onto the backseat and covered her body with his. He pulled his gun from its holster at the same time she did.

"False alarm. I think it was a car backfiring. No one behind us is reacting," Charlie said and drove forward slowly as the traffic began to move.

Brody eased up and looked around. "You stay down just in case."

"We're all in danger. Not just me."

Brody focused on his mission to keep Arianna alive to give her testimony. He could not think of anything beyond that—certainly not how much he cared for her. "Don't worry about me or Charlie."

"But I do."

He glanced down at her, caught the worry in her eyes and wanted to dismiss it. He couldn't. Most likely his own expression mirrored hers. "I can take care of myself."

"I could say the same thing, but we both know this is bigger than the both of us. Rainwater is sparing no effort to get me."

"Then we'll have to rely on someone even bigger."

Her gaze locked with his. "The Lord?"

He nodded.

"I'm trying."

He tore his attention away from her before he neglected his duties. She was so close and yet forbidden to him like the apple in the Garden of Eden. As they passed the wreck site, four Alaska state troopers were at the scene, the back of one truck still lying on its side off the highway now. "This was no accident."

Charlie snorted. "Yeah, I was thinking the same thing. A planned roadblock. It allows his men to check the people traveling to Anchorage up close and personal. I wonder what stunts they staged on the other highway into Anchorage."

"At least there's more than one way into Anchorage." Brody did another scan of his surroundings, noting the thinning of the traffic now that they were past the wreck, and clasped Arianna's arm to help her up.

"We'd be disappointed if they hadn't tried something. We'd really be worried about what was going on." Arianna settled back, straightening her gray wig.

"Speak for yourself," Brody said with a grin. "I would have been perfectly happy if they hadn't tried anything. Ah, the wonderful feeling of serenity. I would have relished it."

"What's that? In our line of work, we live with the tension."

Brody's stomach churned with that tension she talked about. His vacation was coming up soon. He'd originally thought of taking it in Alaska, camping in the wilderness. Now he wanted to get as far away as he could from where he worked. Maybe Dan was right about a beach in Hawaii, listening to the waves crash against the shore. Calm. No conflict. No life-or-death stakes. A place where he might be able to put his priorities in order.

"What are you thinking? You're so quiet."

Arianna's question drew him back to the reality of their situation as they raced toward Anchorage. "My next vacation."

"Where?"

"A beach."

"I thought you liked Alaska and the wilderness."

"I've had my fill of this for the time being."

"No salmon fishing on a beach?"

"There are other kinds of fishing on a beach." He could almost feel the waves wash over his feet, his body start to relax totally. He released a slow breath. The only thing missing was Ari…

Charlie began slowing down again. Brody pushed all thoughts of beaches and vacations to the background and sat forward. "What's happening, Charlie?"

"Two state troopers on the side of the road with a parked car. Traffic is slow. Rubbernecking."

As they passed the three cars on the side of the road, Brody surveyed the situation. Two troopers had a man between them, talking to him. The man was shouting, his hands balled.

Arianna clasped Brody's arm. "That man looks like one of Rainwater's men I saw when I was researching his organization."

He remembered Arianna's photographic memory and asked, "Who?"

"Stefan Krasnov. It looks like he's being detained and he isn't too happy about it."

"I've heard that name." Brody studied the man in question, trying to recall where and what.

"He's been in Russia for the past two years. I guess he's back now."

"You really dug deep."

"I like to know everything about who wants me dead."

This was why he liked her. She was professional and good at her job—one similar to his. She understood his work. If only they had met differently....

He shoved that thought into a box, shut the lid and stored it deep in his heart. It wasn't to be.

"The sighting of Krasnov means there'll be other people waiting all along the road. We can't let down our guard even with only fifty miles to go."

Charlie's thoughts reflected Brody's. It wouldn't be over until the trial was over and Arianna was safely relocated.

The outskirts of Anchorage came into view. Arianna's heartbeat hammered a fast staccato through her body. She curled her hands in her lap. This was it. Tomorrow at this time it would be over and she would fly out of here shortly afterward.

But a lot could happen in twenty-four hours. She uncurled her fists and wiped her sweaty palms together.

Brody covered her hands. "Okay? We didn't have any problem the last fifty miles. That's a good thing."

"Did you notice that Seward Highway was littered with state troopers?"

"I'm hoping that was Gus's doing somehow.

His way of protecting us the best way he could. No roadblocks but plenty of state troopers."

"I think it was Gus." Arianna saw another car had been pulled over closer to the city but didn't recognize the person being detained.

"Go north on the Old Seward Highway. You can get off up there." Brody indicated the turn-off. "We're going across the city. At least it's after the rush hour so we should be able to move quickly."

When Charlie drove onto the older road, he said, "I don't know about you two, but I'm starved. I'd like to find a drive-through and pick up something for dinner. We can take the food to the safe house."

Arianna glanced at Brody. "I'm hungry, too. Will there be something to eat at the place?"

"Probably not much. It's Dan Mitchell's house. He's out of town in Hawaii."

"Why there and how are you going to get inside?" Arianna asked.

"Dan is possibly the guy who gave you away. He was on one of your protection teams. They won't look there because if it was him, they'd never suspect him of sheltering us. Plus I know he doesn't have close neighbors. He's got almost an acre of land right outside of town."

Both of her eyebrows hiked up. "Did the man give you a key to his place?"

"Isn't it obvious? I'm going to break in. If he's on the take, we'll find evidence inside. If he isn't, he won't mind in the end."

"That's stretching things a bit."

"I suppose we could go to my apartment, but I have a feeling Rainwater has someone watching that place and all of my friends'. Dan isn't a friend, just a colleague. I know quite a bit about his house only because he loves to talk a lot. I've never been there." When Charlie reached the intersection with Third Avenue, Brody said, "Turn right. He lives off Westover Avenue."

"It is convenient he was going to Hawaii and wouldn't be in Alaska when everything went down," Charlie said as he went into a drive-through of a fried chicken chain.

Hunger tightened Arianna's stomach. "I'll take a whole chicken."

"I'll second that order." Sitting up, Brody scanned their surroundings the whole time Charlie ordered and didn't relax until they'd pulled out of the parking lot and continued the trek toward Dan's house.

Charlie parked around back at the place. "We'll move it when we get the garage open. I don't like leaving the car for everyone to see."

"He would have left his at the airport so there should be room."

Charlie stepped up to the back door before

Brody and slipped out a lock pick to begin working on opening it. The dim light of dusk painted the landscape in shadows.

"We get more nighttime hours here in Anchorage. It's not even eleven yet, and the sun is going down. That might help us." Arianna scoured the wooded area around Dan's house, taking the left side while Brody watched the right—like a team, not a word spoken. They just did it naturally as though they shared each other's thoughts.

"I'm in. His security system was easy to circumvent if you know what you're doing. I do." Charlie swung the door wide and stepped inside first.

What was she going to do when she left tomorrow night or the next morning? She glanced at Brody's strong profile and knew she would miss that everyday for the rest of her life. She couldn't deny the feelings she had developed over the past few intense days. She tried to tell herself that with time, she would forget him. Certainly what they had been through wasn't a good foundation for a normal life. So maybe her love for Brody wasn't really real. It sure felt real, though.

"After you, Arianna," Brody whispered into her ear. She hadn't even heard or seen him move closer.

Charlie came back into the kitchen. "I've opened the garage. I'm moving the car in there."

"We'll check the house, then we can eat." Brody moved to the right while Arianna took the left side of the one story house.

As Arianna passed through each room, she checked any space someone could hide, and she also noted places to examine more thoroughly after they ate. Maybe they could help Brody figure out if Dan was the marshal who had sold her out. When she went into a game room, she came to a stop a foot inside the entrance. Trophies of the man's kills hung on the wall—stuffed and staring at her. She shivered and focused on searching the place rather than paying attention to the deer or bear over a shoulder watching her every move.

Brody appeared in the doorway. "Did you find anything?"

"Nope, but I see you have a laptop. I was beginning to think all Dan did in his spare time was kill animals and then mount them. Do you see the gun over the mantel? It could take care of a bear for sure."

"I can use it when we go to the courthouse tomorrow. If it stops a bear, it'll stop a man, even the huge one we saw called Mankiller."

She flicked her hand toward a table. "The

ammo is in there and plenty of it. Did the laptop have anything on it?"

"I haven't looked through it yet. We'll eat then take a look at it."

"When are we going to leave for the courthouse tomorrow?"

"Probably as soon as we can. We don't know what roadblocks we'll face. I know when we show up the D.A. will have you testify right away. I want to keep a tight schedule. Only let the necessary people know at the last minute. I don't want to give them a chance to intercept us."

"Most likely there are some of Rainwater's men around the courthouse as we speak," Charlie said. "I'm sure they've been there from the very beginning."

"Yes, but if they knew when we were coming, there would be more."

"Come up with a plan yet?" Arianna strode toward the kitchen and the bucket of cold fried chicken.

"Working on it. I want to sketch the floor plan of the courthouse the best I can from memory."

Charlie placed the bucket of chicken in the center of the kitchen table. "I zapped the baked beans. The coleslaw is fine as is. To tell you the truth, I could eat the containers they come in. I'm that hungry."

Arianna laughed. "I'm with you. All this running from the bad guys has increased my appetite."

After they sat, Brody bowed his head. "Lord, I know You'll be with us tomorrow. Help us to deceive Rainwater's men and allow Arianna to testify against Rainwater, and return safely. Bless this food. Amen."

"After we eat, I'll get on the computer and see what I can find about the different marshals." Charlie took several pieces of chicken and passed the container to Arianna. "I love doing computer searches."

"I'll map out what I can of the courthouse. I wish I had your photographic memory, Arianna."

"I was there with Esther Perkins that first week I was protecting her. I didn't see all of it, but I may be able to help you."

"Great. Also, I have a friend in the L.A. U.S. Marshals' office who I worked with for several years. He may be able to help us delve into who might be the mole."

"Does he know Carla Matthews well?" Arianna tried to picture Brody and Carla together and the image wouldn't materialize. They were so different, but when work was most of a person's life, often people started relationships with coworkers. She had with Dirk and regretted it.

"He isn't a fan of hers."

Charlie reached into the bucket and drew out another piece of chicken. "You know this house is a nice one. Mitchell or his wife must have some money to afford this."

Arianna surveyed the kitchen, which looked like it had been recently remodeled with top-of-the-line marble countertops and ceramic tiles. All the stainless-steel appliances were new. "You're right. Does Dan's wife work?"

"No, she quit her job a while back. They're trying to have a family." Brody finished the last of his baked beans, doing his own assessment of his surroundings. "It seems I remember Dan talking about buying a cabin recently on a piece of land near a lake. He loves to hunt and fish."

"No, you're kidding," Arianna said with a smile. "I'd never get that from the trophies on the wall in his game room. His pool table was a beauty, too. His banking information might be somewhere in the house. I'll do a thorough search."

"You've worked with all these marshals. If you had to choose one right now, who do you think it is?" Charlie took a long sip of his coffee.

"I've known Carla the longest. She's a good marshal, very professional on the job. Off the job is totally different. It's like she's two separate people. That's sends up a red flag to me. I think Kevin is still too fresh and new to be corrupted. He's always thought he could change the world single-handedly."

Arianna rose and took her trash to throw away. "And he's a great cook. I think I'm still hungry and only thinking about food."

"Me, too," Brody said, crossing to the refrigerator to look inside. "Ted Banks is good at following directions, but I don't think he's a leader. From what I heard around the office, he messed up on a detail when he was the lead. Our chief hasn't given him one since. I think he realizes where he is will be about it for him, so if he's got ambitions to make more money, Rainwater might have seemed like his only choice." He shut the fridge door.

"Don't forget Ted has two children starting college."

"From what I hear that'll set him back a pretty penny." Charlie cleaned up the table. "Any food in the refrigerator?"

"No, unless you like eating mustard and ketchup." Brody sighed and leaned against the counter. "Mark Baylor was close to retirement. He was talking about doing it at the first of the year. He was quiet, reserved. By the book. I really hadn't gotten to know him as well as Ted and Kevin."

"Anything that stood out to you, Arianna,

while you were at the cabin that first week?" Charlie sat again and opened the laptop.

"I'm not sure my assessment of Ted is quite the same. I saw a marshal that did well running team one. Efficient. Insisted all the rules were followed. I was impressed with how sharp he was. I tried to sneak outside one morning just to stand on the porch in the crisp, fresh air. Ted was right on it."

Arianna waited to hear Brody's admonishment, and it came on cue. "What if the attackers had been outside then? They would have had a clear shot of you."

She lowered her head, her cheeks heated. "I know. It was stupid but I was so tired of the inside of that cabin. It was day six. I thought I could pull it off, have a few minutes outside by myself while the guard made his perimeter round and get back inside unnoticed. Ted opened that door so loud it startled me."

"How about your boss?" Charlie asked while opening, skimming and closing files on Dan's computer.

"I'd say no, but can't totally rule out anyone. He's up for a promotion and I can't see him throwing that away. But then money is a powerful persuader."

"I'll check on assets and anything that may seem out of the ordinary on the five marshals and your boss. Arianna, I'll leave Mitchell to last. See if you find anything in this house to help me."

"I'm calling my buddy in L.A. then Gus. I need to know what has been discovered. He was going to look into it. He may know something by now."

"Like the identity of the sixth victim. We left five behind—if you count Kevin, although we didn't find him." Arianna headed for the hallway. "I'll see if I can find you some paper to use to draw the floor plans of the courthouse."

Arianna started with the master bedroom, a large room with massive pieces of oak furniture. She found a printer with paper in it and took a couple of pieces to Brody who was deep in a conversation with the marshal in L.A. Then she headed back to the master bedroom to search it thoroughly.

In the back of the closet on the top shelf, she discovered a lockbox and carried it into the kitchen. "I need your picking tools."

Charlie gave them to her, and Arianna worked on opening the strongbox. She found the Mitchells' financial papers and other important documents in it. Brody was between calls, so she said, "Come over here. I've hit a gold mine." She passed half the stack to him. "Maybe we can find all the answers in here."

Charlie whistled. "You should see the place Dan Mitchell is staying at in Hawaii. A five-star hotel. He spent lots of money on this vacation."

"Over ten thousand to be exact." Brody waved the sheet of paper he held. "This is the bill and that's not including the food they'll eat."

"How can he afford that on his salary? Federal employees at his level don't make that kind of money." Charlie continued checking emails on the computer.

"You all do realize if Dan is the one none of this can be used against him." Arianna passed more financial papers to Brody and Charlie.

"At this moment I need to know who the mole is. That's more important. Someone can build a case against him later." Brody shuffled through the stack he had, stopped and tapped his finger on the top one. "I think I know how he got his money. Dan's great uncle died last year, and he received a hundred thousand from the estate."

"He never said anything to you all at the office?" Charlie asked, then closed down the email and began researching Kevin Laird.

"I remember he went to Oregon for a funeral last year," Brody said. "That's all. He got the money two months ago. It looks like that's when he planned the vacation and bought the cabin."

"And had the kitchen remodeled, a widescreen TV delivered and ordered a new vehicle that should be delivered next week. My, he's been busy going on a shopping spree." Arianna put back some of the financial sheets into the strongbox. "If I received a hundred K, I have to admit I would plan a dream vacation. But then I'd save the rest since being a bodyguard isn't a lifelong…" Clearing her throat, she took the rest of the papers from Brody and stacked them back the way she took them out.

Brody clasped her shoulder, massaging his fingertips into it. "I'm sorry. You'll do great whatever you decide to do."

She refused to lift her head or he'd see the tears in her eyes. Slamming the box closed, she locked it then started for the master bedroom to put it back where it belonged.

Brody caught up with her in the hallway. "Are you okay?"

When she kept her face turned away, he moved into her line of vision and cradled her face in his hands. She saw him through a sheen of tears. The look he gave her nearly did her in. All she wanted to do was go into his embrace and have a good cry. She hadn't since this all started. She needed to, but she wouldn't allow her emotions to rule right now. They would divert her from what she needed to do: find the mole.

But his tender touch on her face and his eyes

soft with concern made her wish everything was different—that they had met under normal circumstances.

She inhaled a deep breath and covered his hands with hers. "Yes, just trying to assimilate the fact my life as a bodyguard is over, that I won't be able to use my skills to protect others. That's all I've known for so long. I'm not used to having to trust others with my safety."

"I know what you mean. Trusting comes hard in our line of work. But the more I've looked at your situation the more I realize I'm going to have to trust someone in the D.A.'s or the U.S. Marshals' office or both. Not everyone is on Rainwater's payroll. I just have to decide who isn't. A mistake could get you killed."

Or him. Her heartbeat thumped, its sound echoing through her mind like a death knell.

"I know you'll do the best job possible. There comes a time when I have to put myself in the Lord's hands. Let's do what we can and turn the rest over to Him."

He smiled, a gleam in his brown eyes that seemed to shine straight through her. "You're right."

Kiss me. She started to lean toward him when she pulled back, finally putting some space between them. "I'd better get back to finishing my search, then I'll take a look at your floor plans

of the courthouse. I still think we need to figure out the most likely places an attack could
come from."

"I'll draw them as soon as I call Gus for an
update."

Arianna strode toward the hallway to the
bedrooms, then turned to peer back at Brody.
He glanced over his shoulder and their gazes
connected. Never in her life had she seen such
an all-consuming look. She felt possessed and
cherished in that moment. She grasped the corner edge of the wall, willing strength back into
her legs, her knees.

There was no way she wouldn't end up hurt.
She loved Brody Callahan and no amount of
berating herself was going to change that fact.
And when she had to leave him behind, the hurt
would be far worse than when she discovered
Dirk had betrayed her.

ELEVEN

"Still no ID on the sixth corpse at the cabin?" Brody asked Gus a few minutes later as he sat across from Charlie at the kitchen table.

"No, but they were able to ID Mark Baylor and one of the assailants—a Bo Wilson. He was the body outside the cabin along the side, behind some shrubs."

"He was my attacker when I was looking for Kevin. So they don't know who the two men inside were yet? Too bad the camera with photos of those men was ruined when we crossed the river. It might have made the job easier with pictures."

"No, and the two bodies in the cabin were badly burned to the point it will be harder to ID them. They're looking into Kevin's dental records. He rarely went to the dentist according to his mother. One of the bodies at the edge of the woods had a satellite phone, but they don't know who it is."

Brody drummed his fingers against the table-top. Gus had proven himself to be trustworthy. He could be Brody's chance to get Arianna into the courthouse safely. "We're going to need your help tomorrow morning. I know you don't live that far from Anchorage. Can you come here?"

"I'm glad you asked. I want to see this through. Rainwater's men made a mess for us state troopers to manage today on the roads into Anchorage. He needs to find out the good guys will win every once in a while."

"I can't trust anyone in the Marshals' office, so it'll be just us," Brody said.

"I know a couple of the security officers at the courthouse. I have one we can trust. He's my cousin."

They just might have a chance. "I'll be calling the prosecutor first thing tomorrow morning to coordinate getting Arianna there."

"So where are you?"

It was the question Brody had been waiting for. Did he have a choice? Not really, but this felt right. He gave Gus Dan's address. "Come around back. Although he lives in a fairly iso-lated place you never know when someone Dan knows could come by and wonder why a state trooper's car is out front."

"Will do. Be there by six tomorrow morn-ing. I'll be bringing my cousin, Pete Calloway."

After hanging up, Brody slid the white, blank sheets toward him and began sketching what he remembered of the courthouse.

Charlie peered over the top of the computer. "You said something about talking to the prosecutor tomorrow. Is there a chance he's one of Rainwater's men?"

"If he is, he didn't give the location away because all the man knew was that Arianna was here in a safe house in Alaska. No, leaking the location boils down to the five marshals and my supervisor."

"I thought you didn't think it was your boss."

"I hope not, but I can't be one hundred percent sure."

"It isn't going to be easy tomorrow. There's only a day or two left for Arianna to testify. That narrows the timeline."

Brody tapped the pencil against the paper, staring at what little he'd drawn so far.

"Nervous?"

"I'd be stupid if I wasn't concerned. I'm having to depend on others for her safety."

"From what you've told me, you've always had to—except maybe in the woods when you were running from the assailants and dogs. But even then that couple and their granddaughter helped you two."

"You're right. Rainwater doesn't own everyone in Alaska."

Charlie laughed. "It just might seem like he does with everyone shooting at us. Tell you what, I'm going to wait hidden outside until after Gus comes. Most likely if he's going to betray us it'll be then. But honestly I don't think he will. If he was going to, the best time was when he was driving us away from the wreck."

"He's bringing his cousin who works security at the courthouse."

Charlie scowled. "I didn't know he had a cousin."

Brody's head pounded with tension. "Do you know any of Gus's family?"

"Nope. Never needed to. But I'll run a check and make sure he really has a cousin working at the courthouse."

"I'd feel better if you did. He's Pete Calloway."

"What's wrong?" Arianna asked from the doorway.

"Nothing really. Gus and his cousin who's part of the security at the courthouse will be helping us tomorrow. They'll be here around six."

"Then why would you feel better if Charlie does something?"

Brody hadn't wanted her to worry. He'd do

enough for the both of them. "Charlie's checking on Gus's cousin. We like to know what we can about a person we're working with."

"I agree. I always checked out the people I was working for and with as well as anyone associated with them. I don't like surprises." Arianna sat at the table. "I didn't find anything else here that would help us. What did Gus say about the crime scene at the cabin?"

"They identified Mark Baylor and the assailant I killed at the side of the cabin with dental records. Nothing yet on the other four."

"So we don't know if one of the bodies in the woods was Kevin?"

"No. It seems Kevin didn't go to the dentist much. It's taking a little longer to track his dental records down." Brody wanted to smooth the tired lines from her face. He remained seated at the table. Everything was too complicated as it was.

"I've been thinking while searching the house. What if Kevin isn't dead? We never saw his body. The additional bodies in the woods could be the people who started the fire, but instead of getting away, they got caught in it."

"So what are you saying?"

"That Kevin could have been the mole."

"What if he's one of the bodies?"

She shrugged. "It doesn't totally clear him if

he is. Rainwater has no problem double-crossing his associates."

"I've got something," Charlie said in an excited voice. He looked up from the laptop and smiled. "Mark Baylor. I got an email from a techie friend who was running a background check on the names I gave him before we left Fairbanks."

"You contacted someone about this without my knowledge?" Brody gritted his teeth, feeling as though he had no control over the case.

Charlie stared at him. "Yes, and I didn't tell you because I also had him look into you. I left no one out. I never did when I worked a case. I wanted to know what I was getting into."

Brody returned his look for a long moment. If he'd been in Charlie's place, what would he have done? Probably the same thing. That was why he liked and respected the man. He was thorough and relentless. He relaxed his stiff shoulders. "So tell me a little about this guy. Is he a hacker?"

"There is very little he can't get into with time. He doesn't live in Alaska. He used to work for the FBI and went freelance with his services."

"What did he find?" Brody rose and came around to look over Charlie's shoulder at the same time Arianna did.

"Mark was in debt up to his eyeballs. Serious debt. He was close to having his house taken by the bank. That's until last week when he paid off all the back payments."

"Did he pay off the house?"

"No, at least he was smart enough not to do that. My friend is tracking the money trail and will let me know what he finds. I think it will lead to Rainwater."

"Why? Look at Dan. He inherited his money." Brody had to put aside the fact he liked Mark. He had to be impartial.

"Three reasons. Mark hasn't inherited any money, when he goes on vacation and sometimes long weekends, he flies to Las Vegas and you could say I have a gut feeling about this."

"Has he found anything else about the other marshals?"

"Carla has expensive taste in clothes."

"So if it's Mark, then they killed their informant. That'll send a great signal to future informants." Arianna covered her mouth to stifle a yawn.

Brody crossed to the coffeepot and poured a large cup. Lack of sleep was catching up with all of them. "Gus and his cousin will be here around six. We all need some sleep. One person can rest while the other two stay on guard and dig through info. Arianna, do you want to sleep now or later?"

"I'd rather stay up now."

"That's okay," Charlie said. "My eyes are tired from looking at the screen for the past couple of hours. I'll turn it over to you two. See what you can find about Gus's cousin. Try Facebook. You'll be surprised what you can discover on social media sites." Charlie slid the laptop toward Arianna while Brody retook his seat at the table.

When the former FBI agent left the kitchen, Brody took a long sip of his coffee and stared at Arianna over the rim of his mug. "Pete Calloway shouldn't be too hard to locate if he has an account on Facebook. There probably aren't too many with his name living in Alaska."

"It may not be a public account."

"True, but we can start there and do a Google search."

"This world is getting so small. I never had the time to do any of this social media and now that I do, I can't. I don't think WitSec would be too happy if I had an account on any of the social media sites under my new name."

"Probably not a good thing. Even if Rainwater is put in prison, he'll be controlling his organization from there."

"Sad when we know who the criminals are and can't do anything."

"But you are." Brody snared her look, his gut twisting at the thought of all Arianna was giving up to make sure justice was done. She would be "punished" along with Rainwater.

"Brody—" she tore her gaze from his "—thanks for including me in the guard duty."

"I know you. You wouldn't have gone along with it if I didn't."

Her chuckle filled the air. "We've gotten a crash course in each other over the past few days."

He loved hearing that sound from her. "But I wouldn't recommend it for ordinary people."

"What happened at the cabin could have easily ended differently. You're good at your job. You're a light sleeper."

"I could say the same thing about you."

"Well, now that we've complimented each other, I'd better try to find Pete Calloway on the internet since he'll be here in five hours or so," she said. "You would think after all that Gus did for us earlier today that we could trust his judgment and cousin."

"This job has made me jaded. That's the part I hate about it. I want to believe in the good in people but…" Brody shoved back his chair, not able to put into words how the years in law enforcement had changed him. Sometimes he didn't like what he was becoming—totally cynical and distrustful. He realized it when he thought of Gus's cousin. He thought of it when he heard Charlie had his friend check him out. "I'm going to walk through the house, then step outside and walk around. Don't let me in unless I say it's getting cold."

"Sure."

Brody hurried from the kitchen, needing to put some space between him and Arianna. It was becoming harder for him to separate his professional and personal life with her. He wanted her to testify, but there was a part of him that didn't want her to for a while so he could spend more time with her. Not a good way for him to think.

Arianna looked at her watch. Four-thirty in the morning of the day she would testify. After that, her name and life would officially be changed. The thought scared her more than she wanted to admit. Her future was unknown. Not only where she lived but what she would do.

Then there was Brody. She wouldn't see him after this. She rubbed her hand over her heart, pain piercing through it. In such a short amount of time, she'd fallen in love with him. She'd tried not to. She knew no good would come of it in the long run. There was no future for them. No dates. No watching the sunset with not a care in the world for anything but each other.

Then she remembered that time fleeing the dogs and Rainwater's men when they were going over the mountain. They had paused and stared at the night sky as an aurora blazed an eerie green across it. A special moment she would never forget. When she'd looked into his eyes, she'd known then even if she wouldn't admit it to herself that she could and probably would love Brody Callahan. And she couldn't even really tell why other than she felt a connection to him she'd never had with another, not even Dirk.

Through a slit in the blinds, she peered out a window and saw the growing light in the sky as dawn neared. Gus and Pete would be here soon. According to what she discovered on the internet, Pete was exactly what Gus had said. The man had a wife and two children. He had been working security at the courthouse for ten years.

A little voice inside her said that didn't mean he couldn't be on Rainwater's payroll. But somewhere along the line she had to trust the Lord. He was with her; she couldn't do this by herself.

Arianna knocked on the bedroom door. "Brody, it's time to get up."

Before she had a chance to step away, he

opened the door, their bodies inches apart. The hairs on her arms stood up, tingles zipping down her spine. The urge to embrace him and take that kiss she'd wanted all evening washed over her. She backed away.

"Did you sleep?" she asked to fill the silence.

"Yes. I set the alarm on my watch."

"Scared I'd leave you to sleep until Gus came?" His eyes twinkled. "Yep."

"Only because you let me sleep half an hour longer than I should."

"You've got to be sharp today to testify. We don't want Rainwater's crafty lawyer getting the better of you."

"I'm not gonna let this all be for nothing. You may enjoy hiding out, but it's totally overrated as a form of entertainment."

Brody threw back his head and laughed. "I'm going to miss your wit."

She paused at the end of the hallway, turning toward him. "Only my wit?"

A look came into his eyes that stole her breath. It consumed her. It enticed her toward him. A step then another and she was past the bedroom door.

He took her face within his hands and combed his fingers into her hair, holding her still. "I've been telling myself I shouldn't kiss you. It's wrong. But you'll be gone by tomorrow, and I'll regret that I didn't."

He leaned down, brushing his lips across hers. Soft. Heart melting. As his hands slid down her neck and spine, he molded her against him, increasing his claim on her. She surrendered as she never had before to the sensations bombarding her from all sides. The warmth of his embrace. The scent she had come to identify with him—clean and slightly earthy. The intensity in his kiss.

She could forget everything but him. The danger he was in because of her. The hurt she would feel when they parted. The unfairness of it all that she'd finally met a man she could love with her whole heart.

When he pulled back a few inches, he framed her face and rested his forehead against hers. His ragged breathing sounded in the quiet, mingling with her own.

"I wish we had met differently," he murmured and dragged himself away.

He stared off into space for a moment, and she could see his professional facade fall into place. "The second you step out of this house you will wear a bulletproof vest at all times." He strode toward the kitchen. "Any news while I slept?"

"Charlie couldn't find anything on Ted other

than some loans for his twins for college tuition. He borrowed quite a bit but that isn't unusual with the high cost of college."

"So we really don't know for sure about anyone."

"No, although Mark is still looking the most suspicious. Charlie also looked into the helicopter pilot who brought you and your team to the cabin. A state trooper with a stellar record."

"What did he find out about Kevin?"

"The only thing is that his brother is stationed at the air force base here."

Brody halted and swept around, frowning.

"Did you know that?"

He shook his head. "I thought his family lived in Seattle."

"They do except his older brother and family."

"He never said a word in the nine months he's been here. That's odd. We were on a couple of details together. You get to know someone then. Long hours with not a lot to do."

"Yeah, I know." She felt she knew Brody though they'd met only a short time ago.

He let Arianna enter the kitchen first. "I haven't said anything, but after we plan how we're going to get to the courthouse and inside, I'm paying the prosecutor on this case a visit away from the office. He needs to know you're here and will be at the courthouse."

Arianna stopped, blocking his entry. Her gaze automatically swept the room, taking in the exits and the empty seat where Charlie had been sitting before he went outside to wait for Gus and Pete. "Where are you gonna meet him?"

"His house. I know it's risky, but the leak of our location wasn't him because he didn't know where we were. I need to be there before the police escort him to the courthouse. Whatever we decide on how to get in, he'll make it easier for us. There'll only be three of us besides Pete on duty, to protect you and get you inside. Rainwater will have a lot more men than that. Nothing can go wrong."

A knock at the back door caused Arianna to gasp, so intent had she been on Brody and what he was going to do. She understood why he needed to do it, but she didn't like it. What if Rainwater's men were watching the prosecutor's house? What if Brody was caught and killed?

The very thought pained her more than she thought possible. It had always been easy for her to detach her emotions from what she was doing. That was how she survived in dangerous situations. This time she couldn't.

Brody pulled his gun out of the holster,

peeked out to see who was there then opened the door. Gus and his cousin came inside.

Charlie followed the pair into the kitchen. "I didn't see anything unusual out there. It doesn't look like anyone followed you two."

"At this time of day few are up and about. That made it easy to spot anything unusual. We didn't see anything suspicious." Gus smiled at Arianna. "Good to see you're all right. I worried about you until I heard from Brody last night. This is my cousin. Pete, this is the little lady we're gonna make sure testifies today. I have some good news. Pete is the security officer on the back door into the courthouse today."

Brody crouched near a group of shrubs, close to the deck, in the backyard of Zach Jefferson's house. Fifteen minutes ago the lead prosecutor on the Rainwater case had opened the black-out drapes on a window upstairs—probably his bedroom. He was single, living alone. Brody would wait until the man came downstairs. He knew from past dealings with the prosecutor he was a heavy coffee-drinker, so Brody hoped he went to the kitchen before leaving for the courthouse.

When he'd cased out the place earlier, he'd noticed a police car out front. There was some kind of surveillance on Jefferson, but the man in the past had refused police protection. This time he had agreed to a cop outside the house. For his purposes Brody was glad that was all. He didn't want to call Jefferson or meet him at the office, and he wasn't familiar enough with the man's daily routine to plan a chance encounter somewhere else. Besides, time was very limited.

A light came on in the kitchen. Two sets of blinds opened. Brody caught a glimpse of Jefferson staring out one of the windows. When the man turned away, Brody surveyed the backyard then hurried to the deck and knocked on the back door. This was the tricky part. Would Jefferson answer or notify the police out front?

A minute passed. Standing exposed on the deck, Brody felt vulnerable, every nerve alert, every muscle tense. He wanted to be able to get Arianna to the courthouse and immediately into the courtroom to testify. Jefferson could quietly tighten security on the floor and pave the way for Arianna. He could also ruin everything if he was on Rainwater's side.

The door flew open. Jefferson held a gun pointed at Brody's chest.

Arianna stood in front of the mirror in the master bedroom at Dan's house, staring at herself. The dark circles under her eyes attested to the lack of sleep she'd endured over the past few days. The cuts and bruises she could hide with clothing confirmed the trauma she'd gone through to get to this point. Now she was only hours away from walking into the courtroom to end this ordeal. At the moment waiting for Brody's return from the prosecutor's house, she looked and felt like a wreck.

But that couldn't be the case when she sat before the jury. Not only what she said was important but how she said it mattered, too. She had to make it clear that there was no doubt in her mind that Joseph Rainwater killed Thomas Perkins. And there wasn't. Now she just needed to convey that to the twelve men and women when her body and mind were on the verge of exhaustion.

Lord, You've brought me this far. I know You'll be with me the rest of the way. Please guard the persons protecting me. Don't let anyone else die to keep me safe. I'm trying very hard not to let my fears interfere with what I must do. Rainwater can't win. But I've been in the middle of so much death that leaving here for a new life will be a relief.

Except for Brody. Tears smarted her eyes, and she pivoted away from the mirror. That was all she needed to fall apart right now.

I won't think about what could have been. He's my bodyguard. That's all.

Then why was she fretting that he wasn't back from the prosecutor's?

Jefferson scowled. "What are you doing here?"

"To fill you in on Ms. Jackson and what will happen today." Brody didn't take his gaze off the gun still aimed at him.

The prosecutor lowered his weapon and stepped out of Brody's way. "Come in." After he shut the door, he faced Brody, still grasping the .38 but held down at his side. "Where is she?"

"Safe."

The man's frown deepened even more. "We weren't sure you were alive. All we knew was she was missing. In fact, I'd come to the conclusion that Rainwater's men had taken her and killed her somewhere else. Then yesterday some information came to me that made me think I might be wrong."

"I figured by now you've heard about the wreck on Richardson Highway and all the activity on the roads into Anchorage."

"Yes. I knew something was going on. I don't want Rainwater walking on this. Law enforcement officers have been injured and killed because of him. There were two firefighters hurt, too, trying to put out that forest fire. It's still smoldering in places. This has got to stop."

"I'm bringing Ms. Jackson to the courthouse

this morning. First thing, I hope. I have protection for her, but I want her to go right into the courtroom and testify. The longer she has to wait the more chances Rainwater will do something desperate."

"Why aren't you relying on the U.S. Marshals Service?"

"There's a mole. I don't see how else the location of the safe house could have been leaked. To be on the safe side, I have to go on that until proven otherwise. We nearly died several times getting here."

"Your boss isn't going to like that you came straight to me rather than through him. Not protocol."

"My primary—actually only—concern is Ms. Jackson's safety." Nothing can happen to her. The thought it could curdled Brody's gut like corrosive acid.

"Fine. We'll deal with the fallout after this is over."

The doorbell rang. Brody stiffened. "Are you expecting anyone?"

"My escorts to the courthouse. I have been persuaded under the circumstances to accept a police officer outside my house and an escort. There really isn't any reason to go after me. Another prosecutor in my office can step in and wrap the case up. But the police chief, your boss and the mayor insisted."

"I should probably wait until you leave before I do."

"Stay in here." Jefferson grabbed his coffee mug for traveling and started for the front of his house to answer the door.

Brody moved closer to see and hear who was taking Jefferson downtown. While he glimpsed Carla in the entry hall, Ted Banks' booming voice filled the air. "Are you ready, sir?"

"Yes," Jefferson murmured, "let me get my briefcase. We'll go directly to the courthouse."

"I thought you wanted to go to your office first," Carla said.

"Changed my mind."

Footsteps sounded on the hardwood floor, and Brody popped back into the kitchen in case it wasn't Jefferson. Brody wasn't happy that Ted and Carla were escorting the prosecutor. He didn't know if he could trust them, but Jefferson was right. Killing him wouldn't accomplish anything, and he didn't think Ted and Carla were both on the take. Actually he didn't think either one was, but he'd learned to reserve judgment of guilt or innocence until all the evidence was in.

When he heard the front door close and silence permeated the house, Brody left the kitchen and planted himself in the dining room to watch Jefferson leave. Brody peeked through the blinds to see Jefferson climb in the back with Ted next to him while Carla started the engine and pulled away from the curb. The police car followed behind the marshal's car.

Not seconds later across the street in a neighbor's driveway, a dark van backed out and turned in the same direction as the small convoy going to the courthouse. If that was someone tailing them, Ted and Carla were good marshals and would spy the vehicle behind them and take measures to evade. He couldn't worry about Jefferson. He had to get back to Arianna and implement their plan to get her to the courthouse in a couple hours.

Brody hurried to the back door. When he came earlier, he'd gone through a hedge at the back of the property that separated Jefferson's place from his neighbor's. His car was parked two streets over.

As he neared the seven-foot wall, someone behind him said, "What are you doing here?"

TWELVE

Arianna prowled the kitchen. "Why isn't he back by now? He said the prosecutor didn't live that far away. He should have been in and out."

Charlie shut down the laptop. "He's fine. Brody knows how to take care of himself." He rose. "I think I've gotten this computer back to the way it was. All traces of me erased. How about the rest of the house?"

"Done. Ten minutes ago. Where is Gus?"

"Getting the truck we're going to use. It's nice knowing someone who has a lot of relatives."

"And Pete?"

"Gone to work. He'll be ready for us when we show up."

Arianna kneaded her thumb into her palm. "I just want this over with. I want Brody back safe." *I want my old life back.*

Not for the first time she asked God why she

had witnessed the murder. If they had been half an hour later, her life would be so different.

Charlie's throwaway cell phone rang. "Yeah. Okay."

"Was that Brody?"

"No, Gus. He'll be here in five minutes."

Arianna collapsed back against the counter, gripping its edges. "When he gets here, we're going to get Brody, and if you say no, I'll go without you. Once we get Brody, we can leave for the courthouse from there."

Brody slowly rotated toward the man behind him. It was a man he'd seen before in the forest—Boris Mankiller. And behind him was Stefan Krasnov. Each held a gun in their hand. Brody calculated his chances of getting away without being killed and came up with nil. There was nowhere to run at the moment.

Brody glanced at the van he'd seen following the marshal's vehicle. "You're going to lose the prosecutor's car if you don't hurry."

"We know where he's going. Even if we're wrong, it's being tracked. No, you're the reason we doubled back. Your car is being towed as we speak. There'll be no trace of you."

"How did you know I was inside?"

"We bugged Jefferson's house and have been listening in on his conversations. We've gotten some good info, but today was the best because you're going to tell me where you stashed Ms. Jackson."

"You think?" Brody's gun was holstered at his side. Grabbing it and firing it before both men shot him was impossible. He wasn't a quick draw, just a precise shooter.

"Yes. It's over for her. I'll promise you one thing. If you tell me now rather than after I torture you, I'll make sure she dies fast. She won't even know what hit her. But if you make me draw this whole ordeal out, I'll make sure she dies slowly and painfully. The same goes for you."

"And once I tell you, what guarantee do I have you'll keep your word? I've heard you enjoy killing."

Mankiller grinned, a sinister expression that wordlessly confirmed the rumors circulating about him. "My word."

Brody laughed, relieving the tension that had a chokehold on him. But only for a second.

Mankiller's face firmed into a deadly look, and the assassin closed the short space between them bringing the back of his hand across Brody's face. "That's for your disrespectful attitude."

Pain tumbled around inside Brody's head. His ears rang, and the taste of blood coated his lips.

"Let's go. We're gonna leave a little message for Jefferson. He may not be as safe as he thinks. Your dead body in his bed will get that message across."

Arianna sat in the telephone company's truck with Gus driving. Going up and down the streets around Jefferson's house had produced nothing. No Brody. No car he'd driven. Arianna's concern mushroomed. Every nerve shouted that something was wrong.

"I don't see how we missed him. There's really only one direct route from here to Dan's place. We didn't see him on the road." Arianna sat behind Gus with Charlie in the front passenger seat. The only way for her to look out was the windshield and part of Charlie's side window that his body didn't block, but they had all been looking for the white Chevy.

"What do we do now?" Gus asked, the truck idling a few houses down from the prosecutor's.

"Maybe the man is there and can tell us when Brody left," Arianna said and finished piling her hair up then putting on the hard hat.

"No way," Charlie said between clenched teeth.

"The street is deserted. It's early. We're in disguise and we all have vests on as well as hard hats."

Charlie shoved his door open. "I'll go to the house and check around. You two stay here. If I have to I'll ring the doorbell and pose as a telephone repairman."

"No, we need to park in front and really appear as repairmen. We're dressed for the part. Besides, I'm not sitting here and waiting. I don't have a good feeling about this." As the truck crept forward, Arianna pointed toward the prosecutor's place. "There's a van in the driveway. I've seen it somewhere. What if some of Rainwater's thugs have Brody and Mr. Jefferson? If we sit here having a little discussion about it, they could be murdered by the time we make a move. I won't lose him. It's not up for any more debate." She withdrew her gun. "If I have to, I'll go alone."

Charlie glared at her. "Girl, you're stubborn."

"She's got a point." Gus increased his speed until he was at the house and parked the truck along the curb.

Arianna crawled over a few boxes of equipment and put her hands on the back doors to open them.

"Hold on. The least you can do is wait and walk between us. We'll come around like we're checking on something in the back and you can get out then." Charlie threw a frown over his shoulder before he climbed from the truck.

A few seconds later, Arianna hopped down to the street, her gun back in her pocket with her hand on it. "Let's go. From the street about the only house that has a vantage point to see Mr. Jefferson's place is right across the road from him. Thick vegetation blocks the other neighbors. That'll shield us some while we snoop around."

"When we find Brody, he is going to chew us up and spit us out for putting you in jeopardy," Charlie said.

"You haven't. I would have gone by myself. You're protecting me."

Sandwiched between Gus and Charlie, with her gaze trained on the house, especially the windows which were mostly shuttered, Arianna went down the drive toward the back of the two-story house. At the van Charlie signaled Gus to go around one way while he and Arianna circled it in the other direction. She tried the van's door. It was locked. She pressed her face against the dark window and saw some rope and a couple of guns down on the floor.

"Something is wrong. Even if Brody isn't here, the prosecutor might be in trouble."

"Let's go inside." Charlie removed his set of picks and made his way to the back door, which protected him from prying neighbors.

Arianna withdrew her gun from her pocket

with Gus doing likewise. They stood guard while Charlie worked on the lock then opened the door into the kitchen.

Mankiller's fist connected with Brody's jaw. Again and again, knocking him farther into a desk chair in what must be Jefferson's office. The other thug worked to tie Brody's hands behind his back.

For a second Mankiller paused as he switched fists. Stars swam before Brody's eyes. Krasnov yanked the ropes around Brody's wrists so tight his blood flow was cut off, and the ends of Brody's fingers began to tingle.

"That was just me letting off some steam because you sent me on a merry chase up north." Mankiller stepped away and pulled a switchblade from his pocket. "What I'd really like to use is this."

"Who's the mole in the Marshals' office?" Brody asked, through swollen lips.

"Wouldn't you like to know?" Mankiller flicked his attention to his partner working on tying Brody's legs. "Make sure his feet are bound tight, too." When his gaze reconnected with Brody's face, he grinned that sinister smile that turned a person's blood to ice. "I'll tell you right before you die. That is if you don't test my patience. Now you tell me. Where is Ms. Jackson?"

* * *

Arianna heard the noise—flesh hitting flesh—followed by a man saying something. She only caught a couple of the words, but the sound of her name confirmed her sense of danger. Whether it was Brody, the prosecutor or both being tortured, she didn't know. She caught Charlie's attention then Gus's and gestured toward the hallway where another male voice responded to the first one. Brody. For a second, relief washed through her until the sound of flesh hitting flesh began echoing again, filling Arianna with anger and concern.

Gus indicated he would check the other part of the house while she and Charlie found Brody and the man with the coarse voice. Memories of when she had interrupted Rainwater interrogating Thomas Perkins flashed into her mind. Perkins ended up dead.

Please, Father, keep Brody safe.

Arianna sneaked down the hallway toward a room at the end. The feel of her Glock in her hand gave her comfort. This would end better than with Perkins. Surprise was on their side. When she came to the door into the room, her position afforded her a clear sight to what was going on, and her blood boiled. Brody's face was worse than after he encountered the man outside the cabin. Two men towered over Brody who was tied to a chair. The smaller one, Stefan Krasnov, held a gun but his arm was straight at his side, the barrel pointed at the floor.

Thank You, God.

Then Arianna swung her attention to the large, bulky man with short, dark hair. He clasped a switchblade in his hand, which accounted for a thin line sliced across Brody's neck. The wound bled down his front.

"Tell me where she is and this will end quick." The big man pointed at Brody's face with the knife. "Do you need more motivation?"

Brody's response was a glare.

Arianna shoved down the anger rising in her. It could hinder her efficiency. She looked at Charlie and indicated two, then pointed in the direction she wanted him to go when they entered the room.

Charlie nodded, his gun up.

Using her fingers, she counted to three, then swung into the office. "Drop your weapons," she said in the deadliest voice she could muster.

She cocked her gun, ready for the men to resist. The large man, the one she had her Glock trained on, whirled, rage mottling his face. Mankiller glanced from her to Charlie, who pointed his weapon at Krasnov's chest.

Mankiller started to bring his arm up and back, as though to throw the knife.

"I'll shoot you before it leaves your hand. Drop the knife."

The thud from Krasnov tossing his gun on the floor resonated through the air—a sweet sound. Now if only Mankiller would do the same.

"Now," she clipped out.

Indecision warred in Mankiller's face for a moment, then a noise from the hallway pulled his attention away from her.

"Good thing I brought a couple of pairs of handcuffs along. Looks like we'll need them," Gus said as he came into the office.

Mankiller released the knife, which fell to the floor.

"Kick it away." Arianna didn't drop her vigil and wouldn't until these two were behind bars.

"You, too. Kick the gun away," Charlie said, next to Arianna.

"Gus, this would be a great time to use those handcuffs. Brody?" It took all her willpower not to go to him. Not until the two thugs were secured.

"I've been through worse." His words sounded garbled from his swollen, cut lips.

After both men were handcuffed, Arianna made sure Charlie and Gus had their weapons on the pair before she put hers back in her pocket, then rushed to untie Brody. As soon as she freed his hands, she turned to his legs and undid the rope about them while he used his shirt to help stop the bleeding at his neck.

"Be right back. I'm going to get you something better to use." Arianna hurried to the kitchen and grabbed a towel then looked around for a first aid kit. Nothing.

After she returned with the dishtowel, she went from bathroom to bathroom until she found some items to take care of his injuries. She knew he would refuse to go to the hospital until after she had testified.

When she came back into the office, Charlie had used the rope to tie the two men together on the floor. "Where's Gus?"

"Getting the rest of the rope in their van. They won't get away until we can call the police to come pick them up." Charlie tightened the loops around both Mankiller and Krasnov's legs, making it difficult for them to roll or stand up.

"They look like mummies made out of rope," she said and bridged the distance between her and Brody.

"I think that's appropriate." Brody tried to stand and swayed.

Arianna steadied him. "Is there any chance I can talk you into going to the hosp—"

"Not a snowball's chance in the Mojave Desert."

"That's what I thought. I've got gauze to wrap around your neck."

"You're not going to make *me* look like a mummy, are you?"

She laughed. "I'll pass. We don't have the time. I'll patch you up the best I can and the second I have testified, you're going to the hospital. No arguments."

"I'm fine—"

"If you could see your face right now, you wouldn't be saying that." She helped him to a loveseat and sat down next to him. "Now this may sting some."

"Not as bad as before, when you used patching me up to take out your frustration because we didn't give ourselves up to Mankiller in the forest."

"True. This'll be a piece of cake." Arianna opened an antiseptic swab and as gently as she could, started taking care of the worst first— the cut on his neck. The sight of Brody, battered and cut, knotted her stomach. All because he was protecting her.

The two assassins lay trussed on the floor while Charlie and Gus anchored them to the massive mahogany desk nearby so they couldn't scoot to the door.

"You aren't going to make it. You've got a large bounty on your head," Mankiller said with a cackle.

Charlie took the towel Brody had used and

stuffed it into Mankiller's mouth. "There's no reason we have to put up with his ravings."

Ten minutes later Arianna held on to Brody, and they all headed for the truck.

"As soon as we get to the courthouse and inside, Charlie, call the police on those two guys in Jefferson's house. I'll tell the prosecutor what happened so he'll know." Brody hoisted himself into the back of the phone truck.

Arianna climbed into the back with him while Gus drove and Charlie sat where he had before.

The former FBI agent tossed a phone repairman's uniform for Brody to Arianna. "He needs to put it on."

She started to help Brody when he grasped her hands and said, "I can do it myself. I'm not an invalid."

She frowned. He'd allowed her to hold him as they'd walked to the truck, which surprised her. The closer they had come to the vehicle the stronger Brody appeared as though he'd used the trek to regain what he needed to finish his job.

"Fine." She turned her back on him and gave him privacy while Gus pulled away from the curb.

Every muscle tightened into a hard ball as Arianna stared out the windshield and into the right side mirror as they traveled toward the courthouse. The traffic picked up as the truck neared downtown. The hammering of her heart-beat increased, too.

Dressed in his uniform, Brody sat behind Charlie and kept an eye on the left side mir-ror out front. "When we pull up to the service entrance, we need to act as if we're telephone repairmen. I'm sure there's someone watching. We'll take out equipment to carry inside, but make sure you can get to your weapon fast. Without making it too obvious we're guard-ing you, Arianna, you'll be in the middle. Gus, you'll be on one side. You two are almost the same height. I want them to think she's a man. The moustache should help."

Arianna removed it from her pocket and used facial glue to put it on. "Is it on straight?"

Brody nodded, a smile lighting his eyes. "You don't look half-bad in a moustache."

"That's just what a gal wants to hear," she said with a chuckle. The act of laughing eased some of the tension in her body.

He winked at her. "I aim to please."

The heat of a blush moved up her neck and onto her face. She rarely flushed. She'd learned with three older brothers not to. It only made their teasing worse. That Brody could get her to blush only reinforced the effect this man had on her. But before her doubts and regrets about her life to come took over, she pushed them away. If she had thought of not going into Wit-Sec after testifying, what Mankiller had said earlier about a bounty on her head clinched it. She couldn't risk hurting the people she loved—including Brody.

Gus pulled up to the service entrance. Both men in the front climbed from the truck and opened the back doors. Arianna and Brody hopped down, along with the equipment that would make their disguise believable. Together they strode to Pete's entrance. He passed them through, giving them badges to wear. Not a word was exchanged except what was necessary. Gus cased the right side of the hall while Brody the left. Because Charlie was taller, he peered over Arianna and kept an eye out in front as well as behind them.

Arianna stuck her hand into her pocket with her gun and clasped its handle. Brody slowed his step as they neared the elevator and paused, waiting until they could ride it alone. But at the last moment a man stopped the doors from closing. When they reopened, two men entered the elevator. Brody fixed his gaze on the one closest to him while Gus checked out the other rider.

Sweat coated Arianna's forehead and upper lip. Her pulse rate accelerated. When the doors slid open on their floor, for a few seconds her feet were rooted to the ground. Brody touched her arm, and she moved forward. The court-room where the trial was taking place was only yards away. Two guards stood at the double doors. What if one or both of them were killers?

Another couple of steps and a commotion at the end of the hallway riveted the attention of the few people in the hallway. In their planning for this, Brody had stipulated that Charlie be the one in their group to check out anything that might be considered a diversion while Gus and he kept to the plan—moving forward with Arianna, scanning their designated area.

"A man and woman fighting. The woman slapped the man. Two men pulled them apart," Charlie said matter-of-factly.

Staged? Arianna's heartbeat continued to thump rapidly against her chest.

As they neared the door, Brody and Gus withdrew their badges and IDs. "We're delivering a witness. Arianna Jackson. Mr. Jefferson is expecting her."

Each guard scrutinized the identification then looked them all up and down. Arianna removed the moustache and hardhat, shaking out her long silver-blond hair.

"Just a moment." One guard went into the courtroom.

A rivulet of sweat trickled down into her eye. Her three protectors squeezed in close, forming a semicircle around her while panning the long hallway. The hairs on the back of her neck rose.

The guard came back with Mr. Jefferson who smiled at her. When he looked at Brody, the prosecutor's forehead creased. "What happened?"

"I'll tell you after she testifies."

"She is to come in with her escort," the prosecutor said to the two men on guard at the door.

The guard to her right ran the wand down Gus's length and his gun set it off.

"We're all carrying our weapons," Brody said to the man. "She's under protection of the U.S. Marshals Service. Myself and state trooper Gus Calloway must be by her side."

Both guards looked at Mr. Jefferson. He nodded his agreement.

Back at the house, Charlie had said he would like to stay in the hallway and keep an eye on the courtroom from out there.

As the guard started to wave the wand down Arianna, she reached in and removed her gun. "I'd like it back when I leave."

The guard began to argue with her.

"I'll take her weapon when we leave." Brody stepped forward with Arianna.

The guard frowned. "Fine," he said and moved out of their way into the courtroom.

Everyone turned to look at her, dressed as a

telephone repairman with two men at her side, one with a face of a fighter after a tough bout.

Brody leaned close and whispered, "Go get him. I'll be here when you're finished."

Brody listened to her testimony and his respect for her grew even more. Arianna's integrity and straightforwardness were so refreshing. The sacrifices she'd made and would make increased his admiration many times over. He cared about her more than he ever thought possible.

He love—

No, he couldn't go there. She would be gone tomorrow. He couldn't walk away from his job. He made a difference. He—

"Thank you for testifying, Ms. Jackson. You are free to go," the judge said, signaling Brody and Gus next to him to stand.

The next stop was to deliver her to the U.S. Marshals office. Charlie was to notify them and tell Brody's boss what they suspected about a mole—they had ruled him out. At least they could work with him and hand Arianna over to the two marshals who were to escort her to her new home, wherever that was to be. Although he didn't think it was Ted or Carla, he didn't want them involved in case he was wrong. He suspected it had been Mark, with all his debts.

As Arianna stepped down from testifying and walked toward the gate that separated the public gallery from the trial participants, she looked right at Rainwater. She didn't back down when the man's eyes narrowed. A tic twitched in his jaw.

When Arianna saw Brody, she beamed, her eyes dancing as though she felt free for the first time in days. And yet, she would never totally be. His throat closed when he thought of her flying away to some unknown location. He swallowed several times.

"Let's go. I need some fresh air," she said when she approached Brody.

He took up her left side while Gus fell into step on her right. A guard opened the double doors, and they went into the corridor. The guard passed Arianna's gun to Brody. As he suspected, his supervisor stood with Charlie and two other men wearing their Deputy U.S. Marshal badges. The rest of the hallway was empty.

Arianna slanted a look toward Brody. "Who are the two with your boss?"

"The marshals who will take over for me. They'll process you and settle you in your new home."

"So all this is over." Emotions flitted across her face—from relief to sadness to resignation.

"Almost." Brody continued toward the group.

Nearby, a door opened. A police officer stepped into the hall. The ding of the elevator sounded at the other end. Brody glanced toward it to see who was getting off. Empty.

In that second he swiveled toward the police officer as the man drew his gun and aimed it at Arianna. The blast of the weapon shook the air at the same time Brody threw himself in front of Arianna. The bullet ripped into his arm then another struck him. Blackness engulfed him.

With a third shot, Brody collapsed to the floor. Arianna went for her Glock in her pocket. It wasn't there! Brody still had it.

A barrage of gunfire went off around Arianna, all directed at the police officer by a door a few yards from her. He staggered back, collapsed against the wall and slid down to the floor. The gun he'd used to shoot at her dropped from his hand.

While pandemonium broke out around her, Arianna fell to her knees next to Brody. *He can't be dead. He can't be.*

Everything around her faded from her consciousness. All she cared about was Brody. With a trembling hand, she checked his pulse at his neck. Beneath her fingertips she felt one beat.

She looked up and shouted, "Call 911." His vest had stopped the second bullet.

The two marshals along with Brody's supervisor came to her side. "You've got to leave. Now," the blond one said, grasping her arm to help her to her feet.

She fought him. "I'm not leaving him. Get him some help."

The second marshal took Arianna's other arm. "They'll take care of him. You can't stay. Too dangerous."

"I don't care." She tried to wrench herself from their hold.

Their grip tightened about her. One thrust his face into hers, demanding her full attention. "But we do. It's our job to get you out of here in one piece."

Tears burned her eyes. "I can't leave him. He's shot." *Because of me.*

The marshal in her personal space moved away enough for her to see Gus and Charlie with Brody. "He'll get the help he needs. Now let's go."

Charlie glanced up at her and tipped his head toward her.

Her chest hurt so much it was as though she'd been shot, not Brody. She couldn't take in enough oxygen. Her lungs were on fire. "Please, I need to stay. Make sure he'll be all right." His arm had been a bloody mess and that was all that occupied her mind.

"Go now and I'll see what we can do later," the blond marshal said, a look in his eyes that told her he understood.

She nodded. As she strode toward the elevator, she looked back again and saw Brody move. Her heart cracked. The farther away from him she went the more it ripped until it seemed to be in two pieces—one moved forward with her, and the other stayed behind with him.

"I won't leave Anchorage until I see Brody. You all owe me that. He put himself in front of a bullet for me. I can't walk away without thanking him, and making sure with my own eyes that he's all right." Arianna paced the conference room at the U.S. Marshals office.

"I'll get a message to him. You can write one, and I'll make sure he gets it." Supervisory Deputy U.S. Marshal Walter Quinn sat at the table with the other two marshals now responsible for her.

She stopped, balling her hands at her sides. "No. I won't go until I see him. I'm losing everything. The least you all can do is give me this."

"Fine, I'll arrange it tomorrow morning," Marshal Quinn said in a tight voice.

The stress knotting her insides unraveled some. She'd be able to thank him. To see him one last time. Say goodbye. She took the seat nearest her. "What's being done about the leak in this office?"

"We're wading through the information you all gave us and we're interrogating Boris Mankiller and Stefan Krasnov. We'll give the first one a deal that'll be hard to refuse if he gives up the person responsible for the leak."

"Have you identified all the people found at the cabin and the surrounding area?"

"Yes, and one was Kevin Laird. The person not far from him worked for Rainwater. We're not sure the fire was deliberate. There's evidence it was started by a cigarette. Kevin smoked. We have theorized that he was smoking when he was killed by Rainwater's man. It looks like his throat was cut. From the way the bodies were laid out, it seems that Rainwater's guy was trying to put out the fire, but somehow the flames engulfed him."

"Probably not long after, Kevin notified Mark Baylor he was coming back to the cabin." Arianna rose again, too restless to sit long.

Marshal Quinn's eyes grew round. "We thought it was Baylor, with the kind of debt he had."

"The more I think about this the more I think it was Kevin, not Mark. When we were looking into each marshal's background, I noticed

Kevin's brother was in the military here. He works in supplies at the base. I also read there have been some supplies missing over the past year—weapons. One of the things Rainwater deals in is arms. Kevin wanted this assignment. When he first came to the office in Anchorage, he told everyone he was there to be near his brother, but I think it was more than that. Because your agency staff is small, you work with all the law enforcement groups in the area. Not a bad person to have on your payroll if you're a criminal like Rainwater."

"Then why would Rainwater have him killed?"

Arianna gripped the back of the chair. "I don't think Rainwater wanted Kevin found out. It would give him a chance to turn on him. Maybe Kevin's usefulness had come to an end. I imagine it won't take too long for the military police to find the person responsible for the missing weapons. Kevin's brother may even be dead by now. Things are falling apart for Rainwater. He's getting desperate, especially because he's probably facing life in prison."

A frown slashed across Marshal Quinn's mouth. "We need evidence. Even with the man dead, I can't function if there's any chance a mole is in my department."

"You can get it. Dig into his financial records.

Kevin, in all his youthfulness, was smart. His major in college was finance. He hid his money well, but with time you have the resources to find where he buried the money Rainwater paid him. Also, if his brother isn't dead, he'll be an asset." She began pacing again. "But the most telling thing was that Mark let the assailants into the cabin. He wouldn't have if Kevin had given him the signal indicating he was being forced. Kevin never did. When I looked at the suspected marshals from all angles, that was what made me think it could be Kevin. It would have been hard to jump Kevin outside unless he was expecting someone. Shooting him yes, but not up close and personal with a knife."

Ted came into the conference room. "Brody is out of surgery and the jury is out on Rainwater."

A pounding behind her eyes intensified. "I should have been at the hospital," she said more to herself. Then louder, she asked, "The defense didn't have too many witnesses?"

"No. Three, then each attorney gave their closing remarks." Ted studied her. "Brody will be all right. The doc said the bullet that hit his vest cracked a rib, the one that grazed his head didn't really hurt him except to leave a scar. And the doctors were able to repair his arm. They feel he'll regain full use of it in time."

Arianna massaged her temples. "Thanks,

Ted." She swept her gaze from one marshal to the next. "I'm tired and would like to rest."

They all scrambled to their feet as if they were remiss for keeping her so long.

"We have a place here for you. We don't want to move you but once. That'll be tomorrow morning." Marshal Quinn waved for her to go ahead of him out of the conference room.

All she wanted was peace and time by herself. She knew she wouldn't sleep until she saw Brody alive. There would be plenty of time in her lonely future to sleep.

In an office where they had set up a cot for her, she sat and stared at the floor. *God, I'm Yours. Whatever You have in store for me in this new life, I'll do it the best I can. Thank You for saving Brody. I don't know what I would have done if he'd died because of me.*

The next morning, the two marshals who were taking her to her new home escorted her to a car. The blond one opened the back door for her, and she started to climb inside when she saw Brody sitting in the backseat. She'd thought they would take her to the hospital.

"What are you doing here? You're supposed to be laid up in bed." She smiled and slid in beside him, wanting so badly to take him into her embrace, hold him and never let go. She stayed where she was, clasping her hands tightly together in her lap.

"I broke out. At least temporarily, with Walter's help." Brody gestured toward the driver in the front seat.

She drank in the wonderful sight of him, battered but alive. His left arm was in a sling, a white bandage on the side of his head. "You should be in the hospital." The bruises from Mankiller the day before had swollen one eye and his lips, with a cut across the bottom one.

"I heard you demanded to see me before you left." His mouth curved into a smile for a few seconds, a gleam sparkling in his eyes. "It was too dangerous to take you to the hospital. I know how stubborn you can be, and even if they tried to take you away, I was afraid you would evade your protective team and come anyway to the hospital. So I told them I would come to you. Did you write a letter to your parents?"

She fumbled for her purse, her hands shaking. "Yes, and one to each of my brothers. I appreciate you delivering them to my family. That means so much to me, but..." Her throat swelled, making it difficult to say what was in her heart.

"I'm glad to do it. I'll have some time to. It'll be a while before I'm fully recuperated to work again. I'll probably pester the doctor weekly until I can go back to my job."

"You enjoy your work like I did."

"It's all I know really, and despite how I look, this last assignment turned out a success. On the way over here my boss got a call. The jury came back half an hour ago with a guilty verdict for Rainwater. Also, Walter told me they arrested Kevin's brother in the late hours of the night. He was hiding from Rainwater's men. He'll testify to what he knows about the man's weapons trafficking. He'd been working for him for several years, even recruited Kevin for Rainwater, but when he heard Kevin died at the cabin, he knew he was next. You were right. I was still thinking it was Mark."

"Praise God everything is wrapping up— except for Esther," Arianna said. "Marshal Quinn told me they still haven't found her or her body." She didn't want to talk about the case, but there was something about Brody, a restrained, aloof posture, that told her anything else would be met with silence.

"No, and they may never. But Rainwater's organization is beginning to unravel. Even Stefan Krasnov is making a deal with the prosecutor."

"Not Mankiller?"

"I guess he'll be loyal to the end." Brody

began telling her about the fake police officer that tried to kill her yesterday.

She heard his words, but they barely registered in her mind. She wanted to tell him she loved him and beg him to come with her. But she wouldn't. She couldn't ask him to give up his life as she had to. It was too hard for a person. He deserved better.

She glanced around and noticed they were pulling up to a private hangar. "I guess it's time for me to go—wherever. I—I—" she cleared her throat "—want to thank you for saving me several times. You took a bullet for me. That—"

He put his fingers over her mouth. "It's my job. You know it. You're a bodyguard."

His touch melted the defenses she was desperately trying to shore up. She wanted so much more. "No, you went beyond your job. You and I both know that. You'll always have a special place in my heart." That was the closest she would come to telling him how she felt in person. When her door opened, she peered over her shoulder at the blond marshal. "Just a minute."

"I'll walk you to the plane," Brody said in a thick voice. He swallowed hard.

"No. It's bad enough you escaped the hospital. This is goodbye. I've never worked with someone so professional and dedicated as you." Arianna leaned forward and gently took his face in her hands, aware of his injuries. She whispered her mouth over his, again aware of his wounds. She found a place on his cheek that looked relatively safe to kiss and she did, then pulled away, clambered from the car and hurried toward the airplane. She wouldn't cry until she was inside. She didn't want him to see her tears.

Brody watched her go and wanted to go after her. He wouldn't. What they had experienced was surreal. She'd begin a new life; he'd go back to his old one. Life would continue.

He settled his hand on the seat next to him. His fingers encountered the envelopes she'd given him. The top one had his name on it. He tore it open, not wanting to read it. But he knew he had to. It was her last communication with him.

A short note greeted him. All it said was, "I love you, Brody. Have a great life. You'll always be in my heart. Arianna."

He looked up to see the small plane with her on it rise into the air. She'd taken his heart with her.

The sound of a car coming toward her small ranch drew Arianna to the door of her barn in Wyoming. A green Jeep barreled down the gravel road toward her house. She didn't recognize the car—none of her neighbors or friends in town had that color Jeep.

She grabbed her rifle and waited in the barn entrance to see who got out of the vehicle. It could be a buyer for one of her horses, but she wouldn't take any chances. She'd been in Wyoming for nine months, and she had started to do well with her stock of horses. Although the winter had been particularly tough and very lonely, she might be able to make a go at this after all. Getting involved with the playhouse this spring as a makeup artist for its productions had helped, but nothing would heal the deep loneliness she experienced when she allowed herself to think about Brody or her family she'd left behind.

The Jeep came to a stop near the front of her one-story farmhouse. Its door opened. She lifted her rifle in case it was a stranger. She didn't know if she would ever feel totally safe—not after all that had happened in Alaska.

When the person stood, she saw him. Brody. Shock held her immobile for a few seconds before she lowered her rifle and ran toward him.

Closer to him, she slowed. Why was he here after all this time? Maybe something was wrong. With her parents? Rainwater?

"What brings you to these parts? And more importantly, how did you find me?" She stopped a few feet from him, the feeling of vulnerability swamping her.

"You've brought me here and I pulled a few strings with Walter's help. It's a good thing you put me on your list to join you if I chose to or no matter how much I pleaded I would never have gotten this far."

She'd remembered doing it before leaving the office in Alaska, thinking she might say something to him at the hospital. Give him a choice of coming with her. But she'd changed her mind so she hadn't thought anything about it—until now. "Is something wrong?"

"No, everything is great now that I'm here." He slammed the door and strode to her. "I thought once I got better and was back at my job that I would be fine. I'd convinced myself that what we had between us wasn't reality. That I didn't need you. That my job was all I needed."

Arianna's heartbeat kicked up a notch. "And it isn't?"

"No. It took me five months of physical therapy and desk duty before I was allowed back in the field. But it was never the same. No matter how hard I tried I couldn't get you out of my head or heart. I began to hate going to work. That never has happened to me. I'd thought when I gave your parents the letters I would feel better. That made it worse."

Her thundering heartbeat clamored in her head. "Why?"

"Your dad cried when he read your letter. I felt very uncomfortable witnessing that. I tried to leave, but they insisted I stay with them for a few days and tell them all about my time with you. I did. When I left, they gave me some letters for you. I took them, not wanting to tell them I didn't have a way to get them to you." He halted for a few seconds and sucked in a deep breath. "Leaving them was hard, but not as hard as watching you fly out of my life. I love you. I've left the U.S. Marshals Service. I'm not leaving here until I convince you to marry me." His intense gaze seized hers.

"So you're physically all right now?"

He nodded. "I wouldn't have been able to go back to work if not."

"Good." Arianna threw herself at him, winding her arms around him. "I didn't want to hurt you. The last time I saw you I was nearly too afraid to even kiss you goodbye."

"And if I remember, it wasn't even what I would call a proper goodbye kiss."

"How about a proper welcome one?"

His embrace caged her against him as he slanted his mouth over hers. She poured nine months of bottled up emotions into the kiss, taking and giving at the same time.

When he pulled a few inches away, he captured her face in his palms. "I love you, Arianna."

"My new name is Kim Wells."

He chuckled, laugh lines at the corners of his brown eyes. "I love you—Kim."

"I love you," she murmured right before she planted another kiss on his mouth.

* * * * *

Dear Reader,

I am excited to continue writing more stories about strong women who are bodyguards. But the men they meet are equally strong. It is fun to come up with stories that feature two capable protagonists who can take care of themselves. I have another book planned in this Guardians, Inc. series, so look for it in the future.

I love hearing from readers. You can contact me at margaretdaley@gmail.com, or at 1316 S. Peoria Ave., Tulsa, OK 74120. You can also learn more about my books at www.margaret-daley.com. I have a quarterly newsletter that you can sign up for on my website.

Best wishes,

Margaret Daley

Questions for Discussion

1. Trust is important in a relationship. Arianna didn't trust anyone because of the job she was in and a betrayal by Dirk. Brody didn't know if he could even trust the people he worked with after someone betrayed the safe house location. Has anyone caused you to distrust him/her? Why? How did you settle it?

2. Who is your favorite character? Why?

3. Arianna and Brody were running for their lives with assassins after them. Have you ever been really scared? How did you deal with it? Did you turn to anyone for help?

4. Brody's job was to protect Arianna. He was determined to do that and get her to the courthouse to testify. To what lengths have you gone to protect someone? Where would you draw the line?

5. What is your favorite scene? Why?

6. What would you have done if you had been in Arianna's shoes and witnessed a murder?

7. Arianna had to give up her career, family and friends, everything she knew, because she was testifying against Rainwater. She was scared of the unknown future. She didn't know what she would do. What if you were put in a similar situation? How would you deal with having to totally start over in a new life?

8. Arianna couldn't forgive Dirk. She almost went to prison because of his betrayal. Her past ruled her life. Is there something in your past that has done that to you? How can you get beyond that?

9. Arianna fell in love though she tried not to since she knew there wasn't a future for her and Brody. Have you ever done something against your better judgment? How did it turn out?

10. Although Arianna knew she should forgive Dirk, that God wanted her to, she couldn't. Have you ever done something you knew you shouldn't? How did that situation turn out?

11. Who do you think was the mole in the U.S. Marshals office? Why?

12. Arianna was determined to testify against Rainwater even though it would change her life forever. That took courage. What have you done that required courage? Did any scriptures help you through it? Which ones are they?

LARGER-PRINT BOOKS!

GET 2 FREE
LARGER-PRINT NOVELS
PLUS 2 FREE
MYSTERY GIFTS

Love Inspired®
SUSPENSE
RIVETING INSPIRATIONAL ROMANCE

Larger-print novels are now available...

LARGER-PRINT BOOKS!

GET 2 FREE
LARGER-PRINT NOVELS
PLUS 2 FREE
MYSTERY GIFTS

Love Inspired

Larger-print novels are now available...

YES! Please send me 2 FREE LARGER-PRINT Love Inspired® novels and my 2 FREE mystery gifts (gifts are worth about $10). After receiving them, if I don't wish to receive any more books, I can return the shipping statement marked "cancel." If I don't cancel, I will receive 6 brand-new novels every month and be billed just $5.24 per book in the U.S. or $5.74 per book in Canada. That's a savings of at least 23% off the cover price. It's quite a bargain! Shipping and handling is just 50¢ per book in the U.S. and 75¢ per book in Canada.* I understand that accepting the 2 free books and gifts places me under no obligation to buy anything. I can always return a shipment and cancel at any time. Even if I never buy another book, the two free books and gifts are mine to keep forever.

122/322 IDN F49Y

Name _____ (PLEASE PRINT) _____

Address _____ Apt. # _____

City _____ State/Prov. _____ Zip/Postal Code _____

Signature (if under 18, a parent or guardian must sign) _____

Mail to the Harlequin® Reader Service:
IN U.S.A.: P.O. Box 1867, Buffalo, NY 14240-1867
IN CANADA: P.O. Box 609, Fort Erie, Ontario L2A 5X3

**Are you a current subscriber to Love Inspired books
and want to receive the larger-print edition?
Call 1-800-873-8635 or visit www.ReaderService.com.**

* Terms and prices subject to change without notice. Prices do not include applicable taxes. Sales tax applicable in N.Y. Canadian residents will be charged applicable taxes. Offer not valid in Quebec. This offer is limited to one order per household. Not valid for current subscribers to Love Inspired Larger-Print books. All orders subject to credit approval. Credit or debit balances in a customer's account(s) may be offset by any other outstanding balance owed by or to the customer. Please allow 4 to 6 weeks for delivery. Offer available while quantities last.

Your Privacy—The Harlequin® Reader Service is committed to protecting your privacy. Our Privacy Policy is available online at www.ReaderService.com or upon request from the Harlequin Reader Service.

We make a portion of our mailing list available to reputable third parties that offer products we believe may interest you. If you prefer that we not exchange your name with third parties, or if you wish to clarify or modify your communication preferences, please visit us at www.ReaderService.com/consumerchoice or write to us at Harlequin Reader Service Preference Service, P.O. Box 9062, Buffalo, NY 14269. Include your complete name and address.

LILPDIR13R

ReaderService.com

Manage your account online!

- Review your order history
- Manage your payments
- Update your address

> ### *We've designed the Harlequin® Reader Service website just for you.*

Enjoy all the features!

- Reader excerpts from any series
- Respond to mailings and special monthly offers
- Discover new series available to you
- Browse the Bonus Bucks catalog
- Share your feedback

Visit us at:
ReaderService.com